"It's not fair to keep ~~you~~
of your own home, Wyatt.

"It's just that I don't want the kids to get any ideas."

He turned to find Maura standing there in her long cotton gown, the candle casting a soft glow over her face. "What kind of ideas?"

"I don't want them to think that you'll always be a part of their lives," she confessed. "I also don't want them to think that you're a live-in boyfriend."

Wyatt stepped closer. "You don't want people to think you're giving me special favors."

Even in the dim candlelight, he could see her blush.

He wanted so badly to pull her into his arms. "Maura, please believe me, I would never ask you…. I care about you and the kids too much. But with this situation, I can't see there's any other answer. If you're worried about what people will think, tell 'em…that we're engaged."

Dear Reader,

Here is an acronym that explains why you should not miss the opportunity to enjoy four new love stories from Silhouette Romance so close to Valentine's Day:

L is for the last title in Silhouette Romance's delightful MARRYING THE BOSS'S DAUGHTER six-book continuity. So far, Emily Winters has thwarted her father's attempts to marry her off. But has Daddy's little girl finally met her matrimonial match? Find out in *One Bachelor To Go* (#1706) by Nicole Burnham.

O is for the ornery cowboy who's in for a life change when he is forced to share his home…and his heart with a gun-toting single mom and her kids, in Patricia Thayer's *Wyatt's Ready-Made Family* (#1707). It's the latest title in Thayer's continuing THE TEXAS BROTHERHOOD miniseries.

V is for the great vibes you'll get from Teresa Southwick's *Flirting With the Boss* (#1708). This is the second title of Southwick's IF WISHES WERE… terrific new miniseries in which three friends' wishes magically come true.

E is for the emotion you'll feel as you read *Saved by the Baby* (#1709) by Linda Goodnight. In this heartwarming story, a desperate young mother's quest to save her daughter's life leads her back to the child's father, her first and only love.

Read all four of these fabulous stories. I guarantee they'll get you in the mood for *l-o-v-e!*

Mavis C. Allen
Associate Senior Editor

Please address questions and book requests to:
Silhouette Reader Service
U.S.: 3010 Walden Ave., P.O. Box 1325, Buffalo, NY 14269
Canadian: P.O. Box 609, Fort Erie, Ont. L2A 5X3

Wyatt's Ready-Made Family

PATRICIA THAYER

THE TEXAS BROTHERHOOD

SILHOUETTE *Romance*®

Published by Silhouette Books

America's Publisher of Contemporary Romance

To the family newlyweds:
John and Annie Davenport
Alissa and Tim Rawlins
Daniel and Nora Powell
May this be the beginning to a wonderful life together.

SILHOUETTE BOOKS

ISBN 0-373-19707-1

WYATT'S READY-MADE FAMILY

Copyright © 2004 by Patricia Wright

Visit Silhouette at www.eHarlequin.com

Printed in U.S.A.

PATRICIA THAYER

has been writing for the past sixteen years and has published eighteen books with Silhouette. Her books have been nominated for the National Readers' Choice Award, Virginia Romance Writers of America's Holt Medallion, Orange Rose Contest and a prestigious RITA® Award. In 1997, *Nothing Short of a Miracle* won the *Romantic Times* Reviewers' Choice Award for Best Special Edition.

Thanks to the understanding men in her life—her husband of thirty-two years, Steve, and her three grown sons and two grandsons—Pat has been able to fulfill her dream of writing romance. Another dream is to own a cabin in Colorado, where she can spend her days writing and her evenings with her favorite hero, Steve. She loves to hear from readers. You can write to her at P.O. Box 6251, Anaheim, CA 92816-0251, or check her Web site at www.patriciathayer.com for upcoming books.

Chapter One

Why hadn't she gotten the lock fixed?

Maura Wells huddled with her young children in the upstairs hallway, her hearing honed in on an intruder scavenging around downstairs in the house. Oh, God, why doesn't he just leave? There was nothing down there worth stealing.

The slamming of another door pierced the silence. Jeff and Kelly jumped and she hugged them tighter. Then the sound of the intruder's booted steps passed by the staircase. She held her breath, trying to control her shaking. At the same time praying he wasn't coming up. She closed her eyes and the image of outraged Darren formed in the blackness. Her heart hammered in her chest. Could he have found her…so soon? Her lawyer had assured her…

Maura drew several breaths, listening as the unwelcome guest went into the kitchen, then began opening cupboards. It was just like her ex-husband to make her suffer—make her wait for her punishment.

She'd always known someday he would come after her. Well, she wasn't just going to stand here helpless. No more. If she'd learned anything at the shelter, it was that she couldn't let Darren make her a prisoner again, in her own home. But living in the country meant she couldn't expect a quick response from the police. At least she'd had the presence of mind to call her neighbor, Cade. He was on his way. But how long would it take for him to get here?

"Mommy, I'm scared," her daughter whispered. "Make the bad man go away."

"I will, honey." Fighting her own fears, Maura pushed the kids into her bedroom. "You two wait in here. I'm going to make him go away. Don't come downstairs no matter what. Promise?"

With nods from both her six-year-old son and her three-year-old daughter, Maura closed them inside her bedroom, then crept cautiously to the hall closet and took out an old rifle that had been left behind before she'd moved in. She suspected it wouldn't shoot, not that she could pull the trigger anyway, but she wasn't going to let the intruder know that.

Maura started down the stairs. With each step, she struggled to slow her breathing. A small table lamp was on, casing a soft glow over the large sparsely furnished living room. Most everything in the house had been given to her secondhand, except the black duffel bag beside the front door.

That belonged to the visitor.

She stayed back in the shadows, knowing that if it was her ex-husband, there would be no reasoning with him, but she would do anything she had to do to keep him away from her kids. She listened at the sound of cupboard doors being opened and closed. Then the sound of boots on the bare floors told her he was coming toward her. Here was her chance to catch him by surprise.

The huge shadow appeared, too big to be Darren. A strange relief ran through Maura, then she realized she faced a different kind of danger. He was a thief, maybe worse. She pointed the rifle at him. "Just hold it right there, mister."

"What the hell?" The man stopped at the entrance of the room.

Maura bit back a gasp as she took in the tall, handsome stranger. He was dressed in a Western shirt and jeans with a big silver buckle on his belt. He had midnight-black hair long enough to brush against his collar. His eyes were a brilliant blue hooded by dark brows.

"Raise your hands," she said, fighting to keep the quiver out of her voice, and her hands steady.

To say the least, Wyatt Gentry was surprised to find this pretty interloper in his house. By her state of dress, the long nightgown and her mussed, honey-blond hair, she'd been awakened from sleep. And she looked sexy as all get out. So she was the reason the inside of the house had looked so neat...so welcoming. Too bad the woman holding the rifle didn't.

He sure-as-hell didn't want to talk to anyone holding a weapon at him. "I'm not here to cause any harm, ma'am."

"Then you shouldn't have broken into my home in the first place."

Her home? "Why don't you put the rifle down and we'll talk about it?"

"No! We'll just wait until the sheriff gets here." Her

chocolate-brown eyes widened as she waved the rifle toward the sofa. "Go and sit down."

Wyatt started to walk across the polished hardwood floor, but decided he didn't like this situation at all. And he needed to do something about it. Now. He swung around, grabbed the barrel of the rifle and jerked it from her hands. What he didn't expect was for her to fight him like a sharp-clawed cat. Her small size didn't diminish her strength as she pushed him off balance, but he took her with him when she refused to let go of the rifle. They ended up on the floor. When he finally got leverage, he rolled her over beneath him, then straddled her. She still didn't give up the fight, causing her shapely body to rub against his, reminding him that she was nearly naked and very much a woman. The friction between them was like a jolt of electricity.

"Will you stop fighting me so we can talk about this?" he asked when suddenly something hit him from behind.

"You leave my mother alone," a youngster said as a small fist plummeted him. Hard. Wyatt reach back and pulled a boy off him as he stood up.

"Hey, kid. I'm not going to hurt anyone." He held the small flailing body away from him. He glanced at the woman as she scurried from the floor to the little girl crying on the stairs.

"Please, release my son and just take what you want," the woman pleaded. "I have a little money in my purse. Just don't hurt us."

Seeing the fear in the woman's eyes, Wyatt hurried to reassure her that he wasn't going to harm her or her family. "I'm not going to hurt anyone," he insisted and tossed the rifle on the sofa. He doubted it would fire anyway. "And I don't want your money. I'm only here because I own this house and property. I have a key."

Shock turned to puzzlement on the woman's pretty face. "You bought this ranch?"

He nodded. "As of three o'clock this afternoon when I signed the papers."

"Jeffrey, stop!" she commanded her still struggling son. "The man isn't going to hurt us."

The boy finally stopped fighting, but continued his threatening stare as he was lowered to the floor and backed away toward his mother.

Wyatt straightened. "I'm Wyatt Gentry. Sorry, I had no idea anyone was living in this house."

"I'm Maura Wells, my daughter, Kelly and son, Jeff. We've been staying here for a while…"

"A while. You're renting the place?"

Her incredible dark brown eyes rounded before she glanced away. "I had an agreement with the owner— previous owner. But since you're here now we should leave."

Wyatt had no idea he would be greeted by a full house. Why hadn't the lawyer told him about the renters? How could he toss this woman and her kids out in the middle of the night? And where was her husband? He glanced at her ringless left hand.

"There's no need for you to leave—" he began.

Just then the front door burst open and a tall man rushed in and headed straight for Wyatt. He grabbed a handful of his shirt. "If you laid one hand on any of them you're going to be sorry—"

"No, Cade, please, don't," Maura said as she stepped between them, then reached for the man's arm. "It's okay. This is Wyatt Gentry. He just bought the place."

Cade released him. "You bought this ranch?"

Wyatt nodded. "As of today when I signed the papers." He went to the duffel bag, pulled out the property title and handed it to him.

Cade glanced over the legal agreement. "Well, I'll be damned." He looked at Wyatt as a ruddy color covered his cheeks. "I guess I owe you an apology," he said and gave him back the documents. "I'm Cade Randell. We had no idea the property had sold."

A strange feeling came over Wyatt as he stared at Cade Randell. This was not how he'd planned to meet his half brother. He glanced away, fighting to stay focused on the problem at hand.

Cade Randell turned to the woman. "Maura, why don't you pack your things and you and the kids come home with me?"

Wyatt stepped in. "Like I was telling Mrs. Wells," Wyatt began, "there's no need to leave in the middle of the night. Besides, I'm not going to toss out renters."

Maura spoke up. "I'm not exactly renting...this house," she said timidly. "Cade got permission for me to live here until the place was sold. I guess that's right now."

So Cade Randell had once again been her champion. Was something going on between these two?

"It was like this," Cade said, "I know the owner, Ben Roscoe, and he agreed to let Maura and her kids stay here for a while. I guess when he went on vacation, he neglected to explain the situation to his lawyer." Cade exchanged another glance with Maura. "It's just that this old place has been up for sale for over four years. No one thought it would be a problem for Maura to take the job of house-sitter."

Wyatt had had a long day, a long week with his drive from Arizona, not counting the endless arguments he'd had with his brother, Dylan, about him purchasing the once-Randell property. Now it was nearly midnight and he was exhausted.

"Why don't we hash this out tomorrow?" he suggested. "I can get a motel room and stay there tonight. And we can discuss the living arrangements in the morning."

He studied Maura Wells carefully. Why would a woman and her two kids be living in a deserted house? He didn't like the scenario he came up with.

"Mr. Gentry, I can't make you leave your own house."

Wyatt took another look at her. Not a good idea. She had big brown eyes and fair, flawless skin. Her silky hair was the color of honey. When his body took notice of her attractiveness, he forced his gaze away and glanced around the room.

"Listen," he began, "I was told to expect to have to spend a lot of time cleaning to make this place livable so I wasn't planning on moving in tonight anyway." He placed his black cowboy hat on his head. "I'll stop by in the morning." He picked up his duffel bag and headed out the door.

Maura was thrown by the stranger's kindness. But that didn't change the fact that she and the kids would be homeless in the morning. That meant she would need to find another place to live. Easier said than done. She didn't have the kind of money it would take to relocate and to pay rent.

"I still say you should come home and stay with Abby and me," Cade suggested.

Maura ignored the suggestion and turned to her son. "Jeff, take your sister back upstairs to bed. You can put her in my room." She kissed Kelly, then her son. "Go, Kelly, I'll be up soon."

"Promise?" her daughter asked.

"I promise. You're safe now."

After they both hurried up the steps, Maura turned back to Cade. "I can't come home with you. You already have a houseful with Brandon and Henry James. I won't intrude any more. I'll think of something."

"I have a foreman's cottage you could use. Not exactly in the best shape, but we could fix it up."

Maura had been lucky to find people like Abby and Cade Randell. Between her job and the house, they had helped her so much. She'd never be able to repay them. "I think you know I'm not afraid of hard work. But let's talk about this in the morning. Sorry to bring you out so late." She turned him toward the door. "Now, go home to your family."

Maura finally got Cade to leave. She started to turn off the light, but decided she'd leave it on just for tonight. She climbed the steps, realizing she'd done what she'd promised herself she wouldn't do. She had gotten attached to this house, knowing full well that she couldn't stay forever. But two months had been too short a time. She wanted to hate Wyatt Gentry, but she found she couldn't. Instead, surprisingly, she was looking forward to his return tomorrow, especially since that meant her departure.

Wyatt had been up since dawn, but he doubted Maura Wells had. So he hung around the motel café trying to come up with a solution for all of them. There weren't any answers, especially if the woman and her kids couldn't afford rent for another house.

About seven-thirty, he pulled his truck up in front of

the once white, two-story house. Home sweet home. His first ever. He raised an eyebrow at the peeling paint, the sagging porch, the weed-infested yard and flower beds.

It was all his.

No more trailer, no more campgrounds and traveling around. Wyatt was finally putting down roots. He had his dream, his own ranch. Best of all, none of it had Earl Keys's name on it to remind him that he and Dylan were never wanted, they just came along as excess baggage with their mother. Twenty years ago, Sally Gentry had married a man who promised to take care of her and her twin sons. She believed that Keys was the answer to their prayers until they discovered that he only wanted them to help work his rough-stock business.

No more. He'd worked for years riding in rodeos and working for rough-stock contractors. Now, the Rocking R was his. He belonged here, and never again would he feel like a hired hand. If he was going to work his fingers to the bone it would be because this land was his.

He chuckled. He hadn't come to Texas to buy land but to find his real father. After getting a letter from a man named Jared Trager, telling him about Jack Randell, Wyatt headed to San Angelo. That was how he ended up at the Rocking R. Although the place had been deserted by the Randells, fate had practically handed him the home he'd longed for, and at a price he couldn't pass up. All that was left for him was to move in.

But first he had to evict the squatters. Wyatt climbed out of the cab and walked up the rickety steps and around the rotted wood on the porch, making a mental note to replace them first thing. He knocked on the door and within seconds heard the scurrying of shoes on the floors. The door jerked open and the boy, Jeff, appeared.

"Oh, it's you." The kid looked grim.

"Is your mother around? I told her that I'd be back this morning."

The kid opened his mouth and yelled, "Mom!" Then he ran off leaving the door ajar.

Wyatt took a step inside and closed the door behind him. He heard a commotion upstairs and the cry of a child. A few minutes later the small girl slowly descended the stairs. She was wearing bright-pink shorts, a white T-shirt and canvas shoes, her blond curls were in a ponytail tied with a pink ribbon. There were tears in her eyes and she was making a hiccuping sound.

Wyatt wondered if she were hurt. Feeling a little awkward, he went to her. "What's the matter?"

Kelly stopped on the third step from the bottom. "Mommy's mad with me." Her tiny fists rubbed her eyes.

Wyatt squatted down. "And just why is that?"

"'Cause I got into her makeup and I'm not s'pose to. I want to be pretty like Mommy."

Wyatt had to bite his lip to keep from smiling. He figured Maura Wells didn't need to wear any makeup for that. She was already a natural beauty. "You're just as pretty with your curls." He gave a tug on the ponytail.

She giggled. "What's your name?"

"Wyatt."

She studied him closely. "Are you a mean man?"

He shook his head. "I hope not."

"Jeff says you're going to throw us out." The girl's lower lips quivered as if she were going to cry again.

Wyatt suddenly felt like the meanest man on earth. Before he could say any more Maura Wells appeared at the top of the stairs. "Kelly Ann Wells, did you brush your teeth?"

The girl swung around and looked up at her mother. "I forgot."

"Well, you better get to it. We have to leave soon." The girl hurried up the steps, past her mother and ran down the hall. Maura descended the steps. She was dressed in a flowery skirt and a white cotton T-shirt and wore strappy sandals on her slender feet. Her golden-yellow hair was curled under just brushing her shoulders. No. She definitely didn't need makeup to enhance her beauty.

"I'm sorry, Mr. Gentry. Mornings around here are a little hectic." Before he could answer a horn sounded and she called out, "Jeff, the bus is here."

Within seconds the boy came tearing through the house. He grabbed a backpack and a lunch sack off the table by the door. "Bye, Mom." He threw Wyatt a stony glance and ran out the door.

Peaceful silence. "Sorry, like I was saying the mornings are a little busy. Would you like some coffee?"

"That would be nice," Wyatt said and followed her into the kitchen.

On the way Wyatt took the opportunity of daylight to look around. The rooms obviously needed paint, but everything was clean and neat. Maura Wells had taken care of the place. In the kitchen, she pulled down two mugs from the knotty pine cupboard, then poured the brew from a coffeemaker. "Please, sit down."

Wyatt watched as she moved around the old-fashioned kitchen. He didn't take Maura to be much older than her late twenties. She was small, maybe a little on the thin side, but she didn't lack curves. He watched the sway of her hips under her skirt.

"I'm sure you want to move in as soon as possible,"

she said as she sat down at the table and motioned for him to do also. "I'm sorry if we created a problem."

"Not a big deal."

She sighed. "We can be out…today."

Wyatt looked out the window and saw the sorry-looking station wagon parked by the back door. The woman definitely didn't have much. Where was her husband? He looked back at her. "Do you have a place to go? I mean, I didn't give you much notice."

"We're not your concern, Mr. Gentry."

Then why did he feel as if they were? "Please, call me Wyatt."

She nodded. "Wyatt. We'll probably stay with Cade and Abby Randell for a few days. If it's okay, I'll have to leave my furniture here temporarily, until I find another place."

Why did he feel like such a rat? He couldn't do this. "Huh…that's what I wanted to talk to you about. I was wondering if you could do me a favor?"

She nodded. "Of course."

"There's so much work to do around the place. I was thinking there's no reason why you and the kids couldn't stay in the house." He rushed on seeing her start to protest. "You'd be a big help to me with decorating the inside. And you could take your time finding another place to live."

"Oh, Wyatt," she gasped. Her breathy tone caused his stomach to tighten. "I can't do that. Where would you live?"

"I thought I'd move into the Rocking R's foreman's cottage while I was doing the work. I don't need much room."

Maura couldn't believe it. She could stay. But for how long? She didn't care. Right now, she couldn't afford to go anywhere. There wasn't enough money in her emergency fund to rent a house. She didn't even *have* an emergency fund. Besides, she hated to pack up Jeff and Kelly again. "But how would I be helping?"

"I know zilch about decorating. I'm a bachelor. Spent a lot of my life living out of a single-wide trailer with my mom and brother." *While my stepfather shouted orders from back at his ranch,* he added silently. "I don't know anything about colors and styles and I can see how well you've taken care of the place."

"How much rent would you want?"

He shook his head. "I don't want any rent, but if you could include me at mealtimes, I'd be grateful."

"That doesn't quite seem fair. Us living here and you in the cottage."

"I was planning to move into the cottage anyway while I did the work, so the house will be empty if you and the kids move out."

Maura knew he was probably lying, but bless him, he was trying to help her. She never wanted to be beholden to a man again. It had taken her a long time to stand on her own and not be afraid. But the truth was, she had to think about the kids, keeping a roof over their heads. They loved it here. How could she uproot them again? Besides, she had nowhere to go but back to the shelter once she wore out her welcome at Abby and Cade's. At least, Wyatt Gentry was offering her time to figure out where to go.

"I appreciate your offer, but I feel that if I'm going to stay I need to do something more."

"What is that?"

"I'll not only cook your meals, but do your laundry, too."

When he started to argue, she stopped him with her raised hand. "Take it or leave it, Mr. Gentry."

A slow smile came over his handsome face and a strange feeling erupted in her stomach. "Lady, you got yourself a deal."

Chapter Two

Maura ended up running late for work. But she couldn't just walk out on Wyatt Gentry. After all he was going to be her landlord. She was both excited and relieved that they could come to terms so she and the kids could stay...for a while.

She pulled her car into the parking lot of the Mustang Valley Guest Ranch Center, and escorted Kelly through the doors of the bright red-and-blue building of the employee's day care. Since summer had ended and the seasonal workers were gone until next spring, there were only four other children there.

The Little Pony Day Care had been a lifesaver for Maura. She had very few skills for today's job market and could never have made enough money to be able to afford someone to watch Jeff and Kelly, let alone a licensed day care. But Maura had been offered the free service along with her job. Best of all, Kelly loved staying here.

"Give me a kiss, sweetie," she said to Kelly.

Her daughter puckered up and kissed her. Not long ago, Kelly wouldn't willingly leave Maura's side. Now, she was a happy, independent child.

After last night, Maura was afraid her daughter might revert into her former shell, but she relaxed when Kelly ran over to her friend, Emily, and began to play. So Wyatt Gentry's surprise arrival hadn't caused the child any lasting problems. Maura wished the same was true for herself. She now had a man practically living in the house, and he'd be sitting at her dinner table every night.

"Bye, Mommy. I love you."

"I love you, too, pumpkin."

With a wave goodbye, Maura hurried out the door and across the complex to the strip mall that included a general store and the cabin check-in and rental area for the guest ranch. There was also a souvenir shop, a video arcade, the Mustang Western Clothing Store, then came Abby's Treasures that carried nice collectibles and freshwater pearls from the local Concho River. And last in line was the flower shop.

Maura unlocked the front door to the Yellow Rose. She stepped inside and a wonderful floral fragrance engulfed her, causing her to smile. She loved working with the flowers, loved to arrange bouquets for the ranch guests. And if that weren't enough, she was lucky to work for a wonderful family like the Randells, especially Abby. With virtually no experience, Abby had taken a chance on Maura and given her a job. The few things she had known about flowers had come from Carl Perry, her parents' gardener.

A lonely, only child, Maura used to follow Carl around the estate. The poor man answered every question she'd ever asked and taught her everything about flowers, from pruning to fertilizing. Her mother had always insisted there be fresh bouquets in the house daily. What Grace Howell hadn't known or cared about was that Maura was the one doing the floral arrangements. But her parents hadn't noticed much about their daughter until she'd married Darren Wells. And then they'd disowned her completely.

Maura pushed the bad memories from her head and thought about how lucky she was. She had Jeff and Kelly with her, and even received a salary for what she loved to do. Thanks to Abby's encouragement, for the past few months, she had created special bouquets for the guest cabins, and just recently, Maura had been approached to do a local wedding in San Angelo. And she had appointments to talk with prospective brides about doing two more. The Yellow Rose's business was growing and it was more than Maura could handle by herself. She needed to hire an assistant.

Maura put her purse away in the small office. Grabbing the rose-monogrammed apron off the hook, she tied it around her waist. She went to open the shutters, turned the Closed sign to Open, then picked up the fax with the list of today's bouquets. There was an asterisk beside the cabin number of the bridal suite and the name of the couple who would be arriving this afternoon. Maura smiled. Her favorites were the newlywed arrangements. She went down the list of the four other cabins that would be occupied by three o'clock. She needed to get busy.

Maura started toward the work area when the bell over the door sounded. She turned around expecting to find a customer, but instead Abby Randell rushed through the door.

"I didn't think you'd ever get here," Abby said, her green eyes sparkling.

At thirty, the beautiful woman wore her auburn hair short with the ends flipped up. A pair of hoop earrings hung from the tips of her earlobes. Tall and slender, she was dressed in tailored navy slacks and an ecru crepe blouse. Abby was the mother of two young boys, Brandon and James.

"Sorry I was late, but I needed to talk with Wyatt Gentry."

"I know. I wanted to come by the house, but I had an appointment with an artist this morning. He's agreed to let me sell his paintings at Abby's Treasures. Forget about that." She waved her slender hand. "Look, Maura, you and the kids can move in with us. Cade and Travis will come by later and help get your things. Don't worry, we'll find you another place. It was a crazy idea to put you in the old Randell house, but at the time it seemed the best and fastest solution."

Maura tried to interrupt her friend, but she couldn't get a word in. Finally Abby ran out of steam. "Really, there's no need," Maura said. "I'm going to stay where I am."

"What?"

"Wyatt Gentry insisted we continue living in the house…for now."

Abby crossed her arms. "And just where is this…Mr. Gentry going to live?"

"In the foreman's cottage," Maura announced. "At least while he finishes the repairs to the outside of the house."

"Why would he let you stay?"

Maura was puzzled herself. "I'm not exactly sure."

Abby studied her for a while. "And you're okay with this?"

What choice did she have? "He seems like a nice

man.'' She also had to admit that Wyatt Gentry was a very handsome man. That was, if she paid attention to those things. ''And he's giving me time to find another place to live.''

''Then we'll go looking for another place as soon as possible.''

Maura reached for her friend's hand. ''Look, Abby, I need this time. I haven't had a chance to save much money.'' She turned back to the work area.

Abby followed her. ''Then Cade and I will loan it to you.''

Maura shook her head as she pulled open the cooler's glass door, stepped just inside and picked up the canister of fresh-cut roses that had been picked up by Abby earlier that morning.

''No. I can't take any more from you, Abby. Both you and Cade have done so much for us already. Really, we'll be fine. Thanks to Mr. Gentry, I have a little breathing space. This morning we worked out an arrangement. He's not going to charge me rent, and all he wants in return is some decorating help and…meals.''

Silently, she watched as Abby studied her. This woman was more than her employer, she was her friend. They'd met few months ago at a women's shelter in San Angelo, where Abby was a volunteer. Maura had come seeking refuge from her abusive ex-husband. Even though Darren had been sent to jail for robbery, he'd threatened to punish her because she had been the one who turned him in to the police. After leaving Dallas, she'd moved around until her money ran out, then ended up at the shelter's door.

It had been Abby Randell who counseled her, who'd helped her feel good about herself. During the hours they talked and cried together, Abby confided to Maura about her abusive first husband and how long it had taken her to leave the man. Now, she was happily married to Cade Randell, the man she'd always loved and the father of her two sons.

Maura reached for the flower clippers. Starting with the roses, she handled them with great care as she began to trim, then added wire to each long stem. She placed the first rose in the crystal vase, deciding she would go with all white, representing purity and innocence, for the bridal suite. Maybe tomorrow, she would move onto the passionate bloodred roses. Suddenly her thoughts turned to the dark-haired man who'd burst into her life. Why didn't she feel threatened by him?

"You say you're going to help him decorate the house. Does he have a family?" Abby asked.

"He's a bachelor. And he spoke of a brother."

A long pause. "And you're cooking his meals for him?"

"Yes, and I'm also doing his laundry." She rushed on, "That was my idea."

"And I'm not sure if it was a good one."

Maura understood that Abby was just being protective. They both knew how hard it was to trust anyone, or not to worry about falling for the same type of man and end up in the same brutal situation.

"Just promise me that if you feel you don't like this arrangement, you'll come to me for help," Abby insisted.

"I promise, I will," she said. "Besides, it's only going to be for a month, or so. By then, I'll have another place."

"And you always have a place to stay with us," Abby added.

Tears rushed to Maura's eyes. Never in her life had

anyone cared about her like Abby and her family. "And I thank you for that. You've always been there for me, you also taught me to stand on my own and realize my inner strength. And I think it's about time I did."

Later that day, Maura drove home with Jeff and Kelly in tow. Her son's school bus had let him off at the day care where he spent the past two hours with his sister until Maura closed the shop.

Now, Jeff had time to finish his homework while Maura fixed dinner. She was a little worried. Darren had complained a lot about her lack of culinary skills. Not that they could afford much more than ground beef.

Taking the grocery bag out of the car, Maura started up the walk toward the house. The kids had stopped at the door, but they weren't waiting for her. They watched as Wyatt Gentry pulled rotten floorboards from the porch.

She wasn't as disturbed about the condition of the floorboards as much as she was with Wyatt's lack of clothing. Shirtless, beads of sweat covered his bronze skin, clinging to his broad shoulders and chest. He turned around, tipped his black baseball cap and smiled. Her entire body grew warm, and a warm blush covered her face.

"Hello, Maura," he said in that low husky tone. "I hope you don't mind, but I figured this was a good place to start the repair. I'd hate for one of you to fall and hurt yourselves."

"We're not stupid," Jeff growled. "We don't walk in holes." With a glare, he stomped into the house, letting the screen door slam in his wake.

Maura started to apologize for her son's behavior

when Kelly sat down on the step and announced, "My brother's scared of you."

"Kelly!" Maura was mortified at her child's openness.

"He is?" Wyatt asked as he grabbed his shirt from the railing and slipped it on. "I guess that's because I came into the house last night."

Kelly nodded. "But I'm not scared of you."

"You aren't?" Wyatt asked, studying the child.

The girl's large brown eyes roamed over him and he felt himself holding his breath, waiting for her to make a judgment. He hadn't had much experience with kids. Just the ones who hung around the rodeo. They were more interested in his horse than him.

"Nope, 'cause your eyes don't look mean."

It was crazy but her appraisal pleased Wyatt. "Good."

"You're nice." Her ponytail danced against her shoulders. "You let us stay here. And now you're fixin' the broked porch so I don't falled down again. I got an owie. See."

Wyatt leaned down and examined the tiny red mark on her knee. "Well, Miss Kelly, I'm sure sorry about that. I'll just have to make sure that doesn't happen again."

He was rewarded with a giggle. "Can I help you fix it?"

Her mother stepped forward. "Oh, no, honey. You better come inside and stay out of Mr. Gentry's way."

Wyatt straightened and Maura Wells took a step back. Her eyes widened, causing him to freeze in place. She was frightened of him.

"I don't mind if Kelly wants to stay out here," he assured her. "I'll leave the door open and you can hear her from the kitchen.'' He smiled. ''I wouldn't want anything to hamper your progress on dinner. May I ask what's on the menu?''

She shrugged. ''It's just meat loaf and baked potatoes.''

''There's nothing 'just' about home cooking, ma'am. Not when you've been eating restaurant food, or your own cooking for as long as I have.''

''I hope you're not disappointed.'' She started up the steps. ''Just send Kelly inside if she gets in your way.'' Maura opened the screen door and went inside.

Wyatt's gaze followed the gentle sway of her hips as she walked through the house. Maura Wells did have a cute backside. He shook away the direction of his thoughts. That was as far as he could go, admiring her from afar.

Wyatt had been fitting some of the pieces together, and he didn't like how they added up. Someone had put that sadness in Maura's eyes, more than likely her ex-husband. Wyatt assumed he was an ex—if not, the man deserved to be hog-tied and hung out to dry for deserting his family, leaving them to live in a run-down house.

''Wyatt.'' The little girl tugged on his hand. ''You gotta tell me what to do so I can help.''

Wyatt already knew he'd gotten in over his head when he allowed Maura and her kids to stay in the house. He'd always been a sucker to help out. So he'd done his good deed and it wasn't putting him out that much. She'd be gone in thirty days, and out of his life.

He picked up the board he'd sawed to size earlier. ''Why don't you hand me those nails, Kelly?'' He pointed to the box of finishing nails.

Kelly's tiny fingers reached into the box and pulled

out one. "Thank you," he told her and she rewarded him with a smile so sweet it caused his chest to tighten.

Wyatt couldn't let this idyllic moment detour him from contemplating his troubles. First of all, his new neighbors, the Randells, had no idea that he was their half brother. When would be the best opportunity to drop the bombshell? He needed to talk with the man, Jared Trager, who had sent him the information about Jack Randell being his father, before he made any announcements. Of course, Wyatt had confronted his mother when he'd gotten Trager's letter. And after more than thirty years, Sally Gentry Keys finally told him and his twin the truth.

When Wyatt first arrived in town, he'd stopped by the Lazy S, but the foreman had told him that Jared Trager and his family were out of town. So it looked like he had to wait it out a little longer.

In the meantime, there were other Randell brothers around the area. He'd met Cade already. Would one of them recognize him? Not likely. He'd always been told he looked more like his mother's family. Dylan and he were fraternal twins, and his brother was the one who resembled Jack Randell.

Wyatt pounded in the nail and Kelly handed him another. Nothing had turned out the way he'd planned. Even with Dylan urging him to let the matter go—to stay away from a man who hadn't wanted them—Wyatt still found his way to San Angelo. Not only had he come here, but he'd bought the old Randell homestead.

Did he need to belong so badly that he had to buy his old man's land? Wyatt had told himself over and over it was just a good deal—a great deal. He'd only made a ridiculously low offer and the seller accepted it. How could he not want the place?

He had wanted his own ranch for years. Unlike Dylan, he hated all the travel on the circuit and he'd always wanted to put down roots. A home. The old Randell place might not be in the best shape, but it was his. And with the money he'd saved over the years, from rodeoing and working stock, soon he'd be able to start his business as a rough-stock contractor. Over the years he'd made several contacts in the rodeo business. So once he rebuilt the ranch, repaired the corral and the stalls in the barn, he could begin. He already owned six horses now that a friend was boarding until he had the place ready. One in particular a bucking horse, Rock-a-Billy. He just needed to concentrate on his business.

His attention went to his distraction, pretty Maura Wells. Hopefully by the time he brought his stock here, she and her kids would be long gone.

"That was the best meal I've had in a long time," Wyatt said, scooting back from the table.

"Thank you," Maura said. "Would you like some coffee?"

"That would be nice," he replied, smiling at her.

Feeling a little tingle, Maura got up from the table and took two mugs out of the cupboard. After filling them, she walked back to the table. "Cream or sugar?"

"No, just black." He took a sip. "Good coffee."

"Thank you," Maura said again, then was distracted when Jeff dropped his fork on his plate.

"I got homework." He stood and started out of the room.

"Jeff, you didn't ask to be excused and I think you forgot about your plate."

"Can I be excused?" He came back to get his plate and all but tossed it into the sink.

Maura didn't want to call her son on his rude behavior, but she wasn't going to let him get away with it, either. She'd talk with him later. Jeff had had these bouts with rudeness on and off since they'd left Dallas...and his dad. Of course, he had blamed their separation on her, but she couldn't bring herself to discipline him, especially in front of a stranger.

"Mommy, I ate all my green beans. Can I be 'cused?" Kelly flashed a bright smile at Wyatt. "I want to play with my dolly. Her name is Suzy."

"That's a nice name," Wyatt said.

Again Kelly smiled. If Maura didn't know better she'd say her daughter was flirting with Wyatt Gentry. "Just remember that your bedtime is in one hour and you still need a bath."

"Can I have a bubble bath?"

Maura was too tired. "Not tonight, honey. Mommy has to do dishes."

"Why don't you go on with Kelly? I'll clean up," Wyatt suggested.

Maura shook her head. "No, I can't ask you to do them."

"You didn't ask, I offered." He got up and carried his plate to the sink. "You just need to tell where things are."

Maura got up, too. "Kelly, you go play, I'll be up in a while."

The little girl took off.

"You've worked all day, Mr. Gentry. I can't ask you to do dishes."

"And *you* have worked all day, taken care of two kids and fixed dinner. And I thought you were going to call me Wyatt."

Wyatt closed the drain in the sink and began running

water, then he looked in the most obvious place for the soap, under the counter. That was where he found the small off-brand bottle of green liquid. The room might have needed paint and the pine cupboards were scarred, but everything in the house had been cleaned within an inch of its life. He squirted a generous amount of soap in the water, creating bubbles. "I guess Kelly could have helped me and played in bubbles here."

"The operative word is *play*," she said. "She'd make a mess."

Maura tried to scoot in front of the basin so he would move, but the man didn't budge at all. She wasn't comfortable standing so close to him and stepped back.

"You mean like this?" He slashed bubbles at her.

She gasped. "Mr. Gen—Wyatt!"

He cocked an eyebrow, looking far too handsome…and dangerous. A warning went off. She didn't like the feelings he created in her.

"If you don't want more of the same, I suggest you head upstairs to help your daughter. Don't worry, Maura. I can manage a few dishes. But you have a lot more to handle." He stared at her a moment, then said, "I'm not trying to pry, but in case he shows up one day, is there a Mr. Wells?"

She felt herself tense. God, no. "There is… I mean was, but he's not in our lives any longer. I'm divorced and I have full custody of the children."

"The man must have been a fool to let you and the kids go."

"He had nothing to do with it," she said. "It was my decision to leave, and it was a good decision." She felt her anger building and she took a calming breath. "If you don't mind, I *will* go upstairs and help Kelly with her bath." Maura turned and walked out, nearly running was more like it. She never had much experience with men, and definitely not men like Wyatt Gentry.

She'd be better off to stay far away.

After two bedtime stories and a back rub, Kelly finally went to sleep. Maura had gone into her son's room. Jeff was reading, and he never even looked at her, but with some coaxing, she left with a good-night kiss.

Coming down the stairs, she brushed a tear from her eye, telling herself that although Jeff hated her now, she knew she'd done the right thing leaving Darren. Her ex-husband's abuse had gotten out of control long ago. Although she'd protected the kids most of the time, she couldn't stay and watch as Jeff turned into the same type of person. All he ever saw from his father had been cruel and abusive behavior, especially to women.

Worse, Maura knew that if she stayed, Darren would someday kill her. And her kids would be left alone. So she had to do something, even if it meant turning her husband in to the police.

Maura knew it hadn't been the best thing to steal her children away in the middle of the night, but it had been her only escape, the only way she could leave Darren. After the police took him in, she grabbed everything she could put in the station wagon and got out of Dallas. The small amount of money she'd managed to save only went a little way. And what was she supposed to do for a job and a place to live? She'd gotten the help at a women's shelter in San Angelo.

Maura turned off the lamp in the living room, then walked into the kitchen. She gasped when she found Wyatt sitting at the table, reading the newspaper.

''I didn't realize you were still here.''

He smiled at her. ''I hope you don't mind. I'm having

another cup of your good coffee." He stood and offered her a chair. "Care to join me?"

So polite, but so had been Darren…at first. "I really should get to bed."

"I know, but I only want a few minutes."

Maura made her way to the table and sat down. "Is there a problem?"

"That's what I want to know, Maura. Did I do something to upset you? I mean, if it bothers you to have me at the dinner table, I can eat in the cottage."

"No, of course not. You've been so generous letting us stay here. I mean, you could have insisted we leave."

He shook his head, blue eyes piercing into hers. "I couldn't do that." He took a breath. "I don't want to pry, Maura, but it's obvious that you've had some hard times. I don't want to make them worse. So you take your time. I promise I won't get in your way." The chair scooted against the worn floor when he stood. Then he headed out the back door.

Maura wanted to call after him, tell him the truth, but she couldn't, not yet. She still had a long way to go before she trusted a man.

Maybe never.

Chapter Three

The next morning, Wyatt rolled over on the lumpy mattress and groaned as bright sunlight came through the bare, cracked window, reminding him where he was. His new home. Unable to get back to sleep, he decided to get up. He swung his legs over the edge and rubbed his eyes. He glanced at the travel clock on the table and realized it was nearly six-thirty.

He released a long sigh, thinking about what he had to do today…and tomorrow, and the next day. He was already tired but it had nothing to do with his endless list of future chores, and more to do with his lack of sleep last night. No matter how many times he'd told himself to forget about Maura Wells, she still had managed to keep him awake. He was breaking his own rule—to never get involved with a woman with kids…again.

Memories of Amanda Burke and her son, Scott, flooded into his head. He'd fallen hard for the pretty barrel racer. So he'd knocked himself out trying to win the kid over, too. Thanks to the example of Earl Keys, he hadn't known about being a father figure, but he'd tried his damnedest. In the end he'd lost them both when Amanda went back to her ex-husband.

Maybe that was what intrigued him about Maura. She didn't seem to want anything to do with him. From the moment they'd met, she'd acted as if he had the plague. But that hadn't stopped the attraction. He was drawn to her. Maybe it was the sadness in those big brown eyes of hers, or the fear he saw every time he got too close. At the dinner table last night, he'd felt the tension with Maura. And she couldn't get him out of the house fast enough.

Wyatt never had trouble getting female attention, not since he and Dylan had been fourteen and grown to six feet tall. They'd learned quickly how to charm the ladies. But he had outgrown conquests with the buckle bunnies at the rodeos long ago. He'd passed thirty now and wanted to put his full concentration on the ranch and start his business. He had no time or desire to get involved with someone else's problems. So he would put up with the minor inconvenience for the next month, then she and her kids would be gone.

Wyatt slipped on his jeans and walked to the small and shabby kitchen area. It needed a good cleaning, and a lot of work. He tried to close one of the cabinet doors, and it swung back open. Yesterday, he'd chased out a family of squirrels and broke up several spiderwebs. This morning he would call an exterminator and have the cottage sprayed. Probably wouldn't hurt to do the house, too. He'd just have to make sure that Maura and the kids would be gone for the day.

There was a soft knocking sound. He went to the door and found Kelly standing on the stoop. She looked cute dressed in a pair of blue shorts and white top, her hair in a neat ponytail. In her hands she had an insulated coffee mug covered securely with a tight lid.

She smiled. "Good morning, Wyatt. Mommy says you prob'bly need this." She handed him the coffee. "And breakfast is in ten minutes." Her brown eyes rounded as she shook her finger at him. "And you better not be late." The child turned around and skipped off toward the house.

Wyatt couldn't help but smile at the thought of both the daughter and the mother. So maybe he had charmed his way back into the house. He frowned. Maybe that shouldn't get him so excited.

Maura tried not to make too much of the invitation, reminding herself she was just following through with her agreement. After all, fixing the man a few meals was a great trade for a month's free rent.

There was a knock at the back door and she looked up to find Wyatt standing on the porch. Right on time. Even a little rumpled from sleep, he was a gorgeous man. Tall, with broad shoulders and a narrow waist. Seeing him yesterday without a shirt, she knew he didn't have an ounce of fat on his body. It was all muscle. Her gaze moved upward to his face to catch his grin. Another blush warmed her cheeks.

"Wyatt, come in," she said.

"Thank you, ma'am." He opened the screen door and walked in, then winked at Kelly as he hung his hat on the peg by the door.

"Have a seat." Maura turned back to the stove and the pancakes. This was one thing she could make without fail. "Kelly, go get your brother."

The little girl scurried off, leaving them alone. Maura

took a deep breath and released it, then picked up the plate of pancakes and carried them to the table. "Help yourself."

"Don't mind if I do." He stabbed into the stack, taking four.

She slid into the chair across from him. "I want to apologize for last night."

Wyatt stopped pouring syrup. "There's nothing to apologize for. I overstepped my bounds."

"You have every right to ask questions. You're letting us stay here."

He shook his head. "Listen, everyone is entitled to their secrets."

Maura didn't want to talk about her past. She wanted to move on. But she also needed to make Wyatt understand.

"My husband, Darren...we didn't...the divorce was hard on all of us, especially Jeff. With the move from Dallas to San Angelo, he's having difficulty adjusting."

Wyatt knew that Maura was leaving out a lot. Just the look on her face when she talked about her ex told him she was terrified of the man. That only meant one thing—the man had abused her. He felt himself tense. In his book there was nothing lower than a man who used his fists on a woman.

"Maura, I have only one question, then I'll drop the subject altogether. Is there a chance that your ex-husband will come here and bother you?"

"No! He doesn't know where we are," she admitted, terror in her voice. Wyatt wanted nothing more than to take her into his arms and assure her that he would take care of her.

"And as long as you and the kids are under this roof," he said, "I won't let anything happen to you."

Maura started to speak when Kelly came running into the room, crying. Soon to follow was her pleased-looking older brother.

"Mommy, Mommy, Jeff said my freckles were ugly spots."

The little girl ran to her mother. She sobbed as if her heart were broken.

Wyatt glared at the boy, who looked satisfied that he caused chaos. "You're not ugly, Kelly. You're the prettiest little girl that I know."

The girl wiped her eyes. "Really?"

"Do you know what your freckles mean?"

She shook her head causing her ponytail to swing back and forth.

"You've been kissed by the sun."

A bright smile appeared as she looked at her brother. "See, I've been kissed."

Jeff started to speak, but thought twice when he saw Wyatt's challenging look. He turned to his mother. "Mom, I want some pancakes, too."

"Please," Wyatt added.

The boy remained silent for a few seconds, then added, "Please."

Maura dished up two large cakes, then directed Kelly to her chair and put one on her plate and began to cut it up. "No, I want Wyatt to do it." Kelly smiled. "Please."

This was a new experience for him. He had never cut up a child's food. Maura nodded as she sat down. He picked up a fork and began cutting the cake into bite-size pieces.

"There you go, princess. Want some syrup?"

She smiled at him sweetly, then looked at her brother. "Wyatt called me princess."

Jeff mumbled something under his breath, then continued eating his breakfast.

Maura finished her own pancakes and carried her plate to the sink. She hustled her daughter along, then upstairs to brush her teeth. Handing her son his lunch, she sent him off to find his backpack.

When she returned, she discovered Wyatt running water into the sink basin. The man didn't give up. "I told you, you don't have to do those."

"House rules," he said. "You cooked breakfast, I do the dishes."

Maura started to argue but he looked at her with those seductive blue eyes. A warm tingle pulsed through her, settling deep in her stomach and she forgot all about everything. It wasn't until the school bus honked that she realized she was staring. She rushed off to get Jeff out the door.

Wyatt watched as Maura scurried from the room. Seemed the pretty blonde was in constant motion. He couldn't help but appreciate the soft curves of her backside.

Whoa, just rein in those thoughts, buddy. She's off-limits.

Just then little Kelly came into the kitchen. She dropped her backpack on the table. "I go to school, too. But I don't hafta leave yet." She dragged a chair over to the sink. "So can I help you?"

Definitely off-limits. "That would be nice, but I don't want you to get wet."

"I can wear Mama's apron." She darted to the drawer and pulled out a colorful floral apron and tried to put in on. She went to him. "I can't do bows yet."

Wyatt dried off his hands and after only two attempts, he managed to tie the too-big apron on the child. He handed her a towel and she started drying the flatware, and placing each piece carefully on the counter.

"I help Mommy a lot," the child began. "She lets me dust."

"That's very nice of you to help your mother. And you're only three years old."

Her head bobbed up and down in agreement. "I'm going to be four on Thanksgiving. Mommy says I'm not a baby anymore. That I'm growin' up." She eyed him. "Do you have any little girls?"

Wyatt shook his head, wondering when the questions were going to stop. "No. No kids."

"You all by yourself?"

Again he nodded.

"You get scared?"

"I have a mother and my brother."

"Is he mean to you?"

Wyatt had to smile, remembering how he and Dylan had fought when they were kids. "We had fights, but not too many anymore."

"Jeff is a mean brother. He calls me a dumb girl all the time." Tears filled her eyes. "I'm not dumb."

Wyatt wiped off his hands. No sooner had he turned to the girl than more tears began to run down her angel face.

"Now, don't go cryin' on me, princess." He took the towel and dried her wet cheeks. He'd never felt so awkward and clumsy in his life as he patted her back trying to soothe her.

Maura stood in the doorway and watched the touching scene between her daughter and Wyatt Gentry. Kelly had never known the gentleness of a man. Her own father had never wanted her around. So Maura had done everything to keep out of his way. She was surprised that her daughter would seek a man's attention.

Just then Wyatt looked at her and their eyes locked. A spark of desire shot through her and she wondered what it would be like to have this man's arms around her.

Just as quickly the moment ended. "Kelly, look, your mother's here."

The child suddenly brightened. "Mommy, I'm helping Wyatt do the dishes."

"I can see that." She walked to the sink and asked her daughter, "Are you okay?"

Kelly nodded. "Jeff hurt my feelings."

"I'll talk to him after school."

Maura saw Wyatt tense. She knew her son's behavior wasn't perfect, but he'd gone through a lot in the past months. She would deal with it...later.

"It's time to leave for work."

"Okay," Kelly said as she climbed off the stool, then looked up at Wyatt. "I liked helpin' you."

"Thank you, princess. See ya after school." He waved as she started out the back door.

Maura braced herself for Wyatt's criticism for her not disciplining her son, but he didn't say a word.

"If it's okay with you," he began, "I'm going to have an exterminator out to spray the place."

"How long will we have to be out?" she asked.

"I'm hoping I can get someone out today, tomorrow at the latest. At any rate you should be able to come into the house the same evening."

How considerate. There was a kindness that showed in his eyes, along with something else that she didn't want to examine. He looked strong and dangerously masculine. Maura felt a shiver of awareness and realized she was a little breathless. "I'd appreciate that," she managed to say.

"So you won't mind if I use my key?" he asked.

"Of course not. It's your house," she said.

"No, it's *your* house for the time being. I won't come in here unless you say so." He studied her for a moment. "I realize you don't know me very well and I guess that's my fault. There's not much to tell, though. I was born Wyatt Alan Gentry thirty-one years ago, five minutes before my twin brother, Dylan." He cocked an eyebrow at her. "He claims he's the good-looking one. I've lived on a ranch outside Tucson, Arizona, all my life. My mother is Sally and my stepfather is Earl Keys. They've been a rough-stock contractor to the rodeos for years. So most of our lives were spent traveling around Arizona and California. Most of the time we lived out of a trailer."

"It must have been crowded." Maura had lived in a mansion growing up, and had been so lonely.

He tossed her one of those easy grins. "That's one of the reasons I bought this ranch. I got tired of traveling. So I plan to stay put. My goal is to board and train rodeo stock here, hoping when Dylan retires from bull riding he'll join me." He sighed. "That's about it. Unless you want some references, then you can call any rodeo grounds from Arizona through southern California. They'll vouch for the Gentrys."

Wyatt held his breath while Maura took her time studying his face. She looked so pretty in her crisp white blouse and bright flowered skirt. Her blond hair shimmered as she tugged the long strands behind her ears.

"You don't need to provide me with any references," she insisted.

"I don't want you to feel uncomfortable with me around. Like I said, I can eat in the foreman's cottage."

"I'm not uncomfortable," she said. They both knew she was lying. "And you'll eat your meals—at this table—with us. That's our arrangement."

He folded his arms across his chest and peered back at her. "What about you?" he asked. "Where you from? Your accent doesn't ring native Texan."

She shook her head. "I'm originally from the east, New York State. I've been here for nearly eight years, but we've moved a lot…" Her gaze moved around the room, anywhere but at him. "I should get to work." She pulled her car keys out of her purse and headed for the door. "Speaking of our agreement, just let me know when you want to discuss any ideas or color scheme. I could help you with the painting inside."

"I still have so much to do outside," he said. "I need to get the place repaired and painted before winter gets here. But I would like to hear some of your suggestions for the inside of the house."

She nodded. "I'll be home around five-thirty. Any suggestions on supper?"

He smiled. "Surprise me."

For the first time she returned his smile. "Oh, it will definitely be that. See you tonight." She turned and walked out.

Wyatt realized that he was looking forward to when she came home, to seeing her again.

That was not good.

Just as Maura had said, she and the kids arrived home about five-thirty as he worked tightening the hinges on the screen door.

Jeff was the first out of the car. He ran up to the porch without even a word of greeting.

Not Kelly. She jumped out of the car, smiling. "Hi, Wyatt." She took off her backpack and pulled out a piece of paper, the corners a little bent. "See what I made today? A picture. That's you." She pointed to the colorful rough stick figure on the page.

"Really? You made a picture of me?"

She nodded proudly.

"No one has ever drawn me a picture. Thank you."

She twisted her fingers together. "You're welcome."

"Where should we put this? How about on the refrigerator? That way I can see it every day when I eat."

"Okay, I can hang it up for you."

With a grocery bag in her hands, Maura climbed out of the car. Wyatt knew she was shopping for extras with him there. She made her way up the steps and looked around at the progress he'd made. He'd replaced nearly a third of the porch in front of the door. He was now working on the broken railing.

"You've gotten a lot done," she said. "It's going to look nice."

Wyatt felt his body warm with her words, realizing he'd wanted her approval. "Thanks. It was a lot of work, but this old house is worth it."

"It is a wonderful house, just neglected. Except for the roof, it's new," she said. "Cade said that was the one thing I didn't have to worry about when it rained. The house had been built by his grandfather."

"So Cade Randell grew up here. Why doesn't he live here now?"

Maura brushed her hair from her face. "He told me after his mother died there weren't many good memories left. Anyway, his father went to prison and the state confiscated the property and sold it at auction for back taxes. He and his brothers had to go into foster care.''

Wyatt knew little about the Randells, just a few sketchy details from Trager's letter. He tried to act nonchalant, but news about his so-called father being in prison caught him off guard. He'd known that good old Jack hadn't been a man of honor, but he never thought about him as a lawbreaker.

''So Cade and his father aren't close?'' he asked.

Maura shook her head. ''Abby says the man hasn't been back here in years. Just as well, if you ask any of the Randells. Of course the brothers ended up better off. That's how they connected with Hank Barrett. The man took them in and raised them on the Circle B Ranch. The Mustang Valley Guest Ranch is part of Hank's property. It also borders with Abby and Cade's ranch, and with Dana and Jared Trager's. Then there's Chance and Joy. He runs a horse breeding ranch that is on the other side of the Circle B. They run the Mustang Valley Lake and Campground. Travis and Josie live on a section of Hank's land close to the valley. Travis manages the guest ranch.''

Wyatt still couldn't believe it. He had four brothers, and three of them he'd never met. ''It sounds confusing.''

''Their family is large.'' She smiled. ''It must be wonderful to have so many siblings…and nieces and nephews. And there's still more coming. Joy is expecting a baby in a few months.''

Wyatt wondered if he were man enough to face the Randells. Would they accept him? Would he fit in here? He realized that as much as he loved his brother and mother, he needed to find out about his father, the missing piece of himself.

Dylan didn't have this problem. If the decision were up to Wyatt's twin, he'd forget about finding a family, and an old man who never wanted his bastard sons. His brother didn't need or want anything to do with Jack Randell.

Maura's sudden cry drew his attention. He swung around just in time to catch her as she stumbled over a piece of wood. He wrapped his arms around her slender waist and lifted her easily out of harm's way. He set her down beside the railing, but didn't step back. He couldn't. Those big brown eyes of hers locked with his, sending his pulse racing. His breathing suddenly became labored.

"You all right?" he managed to ask.

She nodded and looked down at the crushed bag clutched at her chest. "The groceries seemed to have survived. Barely."

"Good."

They continued to stand there until Maura finally spoke, "Well, I guess I should start supper."

"What's on the menu tonight?"

"Chicken," she said. "Please tell me you like chicken."

"Fried, roasted or grilled, I love chicken."

"You're an easy man to please."

He shrugged. "Some things aren't worth getting upset about. I save my anger for important things."

She started to go inside, but stopped. "Oh, speaking of the Randells, Abby and Cade and the rest of the family have invited us to a barbecue tomorrow night at the Circle B. It's sort of a welcome to San Angelo." She tilted her head a little, looking sweet and sexy at the same time. "If you don't want to go, that's okay…"

"No, I think it's time that I meet the rest of my…neighbors." Wyatt just hoped that they were ready to meet him.

The next evening Wyatt drove them over in his truck, putting the kids in the roomy back seat. Maura sat in the front, feeling strange sitting next to this man. Correction. This good-looking man in his sharply pressed Wrangler jeans and starched tan Western shirt. His brown boots were polished and his tan Resistol cowboy hat sat low on his head.

He was pure cowboy.

And she had no doubt that the Randells would think about pairing her off with Wyatt. The last thing she wanted was for any of them to think he was her date. Why was it always the happily married couples that wanted you to find that perfect mate?

Well, Maura didn't want to find a man. She wasn't even looking. Besides, she wasn't foolish enough to think a man like Wyatt would give her a second look. She gazed down at her own clothes, a pair of discount store jeans and a plain red sleeveless blouse. She was pleasant looking, but certainly not exciting…and she had two kids. Most men would run in the other direction. Wyatt Gentry hadn't had a choice. She was living in his house, but soon would be leaving. But to where?

To a place Darren would never find her or the kids.

When Wyatt drove under the Circle B archway he felt himself becoming a little nervous. He was about to meet his family. And although he'd only been here a few days, it bothered him that he hadn't told Cade who he was. How would they receive him if they knew, especially now that he had purchased their former family home?

He glanced around the impressive ranch, including the pristine white outer buildings and miles of well-kept fence that penned some beautiful horseflesh. He watched as three mustang ponies galloped around the pasture. Then the large two-story house came into view.

"Well, we're here," Maura announced. "Just park over by the other trucks at the barn."

Wyatt pulled in and climbed out, allowing Jeff and Kelly to exit the cab. Maura came around carrying the cake she'd baked for tonight.

"You'll like the Randells." She smiled. "They're the best people. And Hank is a sweet man."

"Still, I'm the stranger here. And I just bought their childhood home."

"If Chance, Cade or Travis would have wanted the ranch, they could have easily bought it."

"You finally made it." A tall, beautiful woman came toward them. Smiling, she hugged Maura, then turned her attention to him. "You must be Wyatt Gentry."

"Yes, ma'am, I am." He shook her hand.

"Welcome to Texas and the Circle B. I'm Abby Randell. I hear you've already met my husband, Cade."

"Briefly."

"That's the best way to meet this family—in small doses. Oh, no, here they all come."

One by one, Abby introduced them—Chance and Joy, Travis and Josie. Then came an older man, tall, straight-backed with thick white hair and friendly hazel eyes. "And this is Hank Barrett."

The man stepped up to him. "Glad you could make it, son."

"Thank you, sir. You have quite a place here."

"Anytime you'd like, I'll show you around."

"I'll keep that in mind."

"How about tomorrow?" Hank suggested. "Come by and we'll saddle up a couple of horses and ride out."

The older man frowned. "Unless you're too busy. I hear you're puttin' in a lot of work on your place."

"I think I can take a few hours off."

The group broke into laughter. But Wyatt noticed Hank was studying him…closely.

"You say you're from Arizona?"

"Tucson." Wyatt was telling the truth, but it bothered him the part he was holding back. If only Jared Trager were here.

Before Maura could protest, she was whisked off to the kitchen to help the other women. The Circle B's housekeeper, Ella, was busy arranging the carry-in food for tonight's party. The tall, older woman had been around at the ranch for years and had had a big hand in raising the boys. Chance, Cade and Travis loved her like a second mother. All the kids thought of her as their grandmother.

"That's one good-looking cowboy you brought with you," Ella whispered to Maura.

"He is?" Maura said, trying to act nonchalant. "I hadn't noticed."

"Sweetie, you'd have to be dead not to notice that man," Ella said. "I'd say he fits right in with all those other tall, dark and handsome boys out there."

Joy came up to the counter carrying a bowl of potato salad. "Well, it wouldn't be the first time," she said. "That was the way with Jared Trager. He first came here to find his deceased brother's son and ended up marrying Dana Shane from the Lazy S Ranch and adopting her son, Evan. Of course, when Jared claimed to be Jack Randell's son, it was not without resistance from Chance, Cade and Travis. They'd even insisted on a DNA test to prove Jared was blood. Even after their rocky start, he fits into the family just fine."

Ella looked at Joy. "When are Jared and Dana supposed to get back from Las Vegas?"

"Dana called me yesterday," Joy said. "She said tomorrow at the latest. I hope so. She's doing fine with the pregnancy, but I miss her." She patted her own extended belly. Her baby was due in a few months. "She's going to be sorry she's missed everything going on around here."

"No, she's not," Abby said pointing out the window. "Because Dana and Jared just drove up."

The women dropped what they were doing and headed out the door to greet the family members who'd been gone for the past two weeks. Joy hugged Dana, then everyone took turns going after Jared, then six-year-old Evan.

"You'd think we were lost in the desert," Jared said, but eagerly accepted a kiss from Ella.

"The last I heard, Las Vegas *is* the desert. Glad to have you all back."

The men arrived by now and they shook hands. It was Cade who stepped up and introduced Wyatt.

"Jared, Dana and Evan, we want you to meet Wyatt Gentry, our new neighbor. He bought the Rocking R. Wyatt, this is our other brother number four, Jared."

Wyatt stepped up and shook Jared's hand, not missing his shocked look.

"That was fast," Jared said. "How come you never called or wrote back? How long have you been here?"

"Thought it would be better just to show up."

All the brothers exchanged glances. "You two know each other?" Cade finally asked.

"Well, sort of," Jared said. "I wrote to Wyatt and his brother, Dylan. It seems that years ago, their mother, Sally Gentry, knew…Jack."

Chapter Four

"You can't be saying what I think you're saying," Cade said, his gaze darting from Wyatt to Jared, then back again.

Jared nodded slowly. "Wyatt Gentry is our half brother," he said.

Everyone in the group grew silent as if waiting for further explanation. Wyatt felt their expectant gazes burning into him. He knew he should speak. The Randells had every right to hear about the circumstances of his birth.

But it was Jared who began. "I got the news a few months ago when Graham Hastings came to see Evan. At first, I thought that the old man was just trying to get back at me for not letting him see his grandson, but then…"

"What exactly did he tell you?" Cade demanded as he placed his hands on his hips, his brothers, Chance and Travis, flanking him. They were all waiting for an answer.

"GH didn't say much. Just that I wasn't Jack Randell's only bastard. Then he gave me a packet from a private investigator with a picture of Jack with a woman named Sally Gentry. Maybe I should have shown it to you all, but I decided it would be best to first contact Wyatt and Dylan—"

"Dylan?" Chance interrupted. "Who the hell is Dylan?"

"He's my twin brother," Wyatt answered, hearing his pulse pounding in his ears.

A mumbled curse came from Cade, then he said, "Hope you didn't come here to collect anything from your daddy," he said, sarcasm lacing in his tone. "You're sh—out of luck."

"Cade!" Abby gasped as she appeared at her husband's side. "Let Wyatt talk."

Cade raised his hands. "I don't want to hear any more about Jack Randell's sins." He turned and marched through the crowd, off toward the house.

Jared came up to Wyatt. "I think it might be a good idea to give them some time to let this news settle in."

Wyatt nodded. Never had he felt like this. All alone. Every other time, he'd had Dylan with him and they handled rejection together. They'd fought their battles side by side. Not tonight. "I'll go."

"I'm sorry," Jared said. "We'll talk soon."

"Sure," Wyatt said and strode off.

Maura watched Wyatt start off toward the truck, his shoulders squared, his head held high. He was definitely a Randell. Why hadn't she seen the resemblance? Tall, dark and with the same good looks as his brothers. One difference, he was alone.

She gathered Jeff and Kelly and followed after him.

Abby stopped her. "Maura, maybe it would be best if you and the kids stay here."

"Why?" she asked, her gaze on Wyatt as he climbed into the cab. "Wyatt Gentry is the same man he was this morning," she said. "He can't help who his parents are."

"You're right," her friend finally agreed. She hugged Maura. "Be careful. You're vulnerable...and so is he. Tell Wyatt that Cade will come around and so will his brothers. They just need some time."

Maura said goodbye and rushed her complaining kids toward Wyatt's truck. She called to him as he was backing out.

He stopped, then peered through the open window.

She picked up her pace. "You can't leave without us."

He looked surprised, then confused. "I just figured you'd want to stay."

She shook her head. "No, the kids have school tomorrow. May we get a ride back with you?"

"Are you sure?"

"I'm sure." Maura walked around to the passenger side and helped the kids inside. She climbed in the front seat and Wyatt took off down the road toward the highway.

"Mom, what about supper?" Jeff whined and crossed his arms over his chest. "Aren't we going to eat?"

"I'll fix you something when we get hom...to the house," she began. She couldn't call the ranch her home. They were going to be gone soon.

"How about I treat everyone to hamburgers, or pizza?" Wyatt suggested.

"You don't have to do that," Maura said sending her

children a stern look as they cheered for pizza. "I have food at the house."

"I know, but Kelly and Jeff had to leave their friends." He glanced away from the road to look at her, his blue eyes sad. "Let me do this, Maura."

She found she wanted to reach out to Wyatt and let him know that it didn't make any difference to her who his parents were. "I guess it's still early and we do have to eat. And pizza does sound good."

Both Kelly and Jeff cheered again, then sat quietly until they pulled into the parking lot of the Pizza Palace. Wyatt walked around the truck and helped Maura out of the cab, surprising her when he gripped her around the waist and lifted her down. His touch was strong, yet gentle and lingered even after he set her on the ground. He tossed her a wink that sent her heart racing. Then just as quickly, he turned away to assist her children.

Inside the restaurant the ringing and beeping sound of video games filled the large room along with the aroma of oregano and pepperoni. After a short discussion they decided on toppings for the pizza. Then before Maura realized what Wyatt was doing, he took some bills from the front pocket of his jeans. He held out two dollars toward Kelly.

"This is for helping me yesterday."

Her eyes rounded as she accepted the money. "Thank you, Wyatt."

He turned to Jeff and held out two more dollars between his fingers. "These are for you, Jeff...if you help watch your sister play her game and if, I can count on your help tomorrow for about an hour."

Maura watched her son stew over the decision. "What do I hafta to do tomorrow?" the boy asked.

"Help with some cleanup," Wyatt said. "And maybe

if you get that finished you can swing a hammer at a few nails. And if it doesn't interfere with your other chores, I could use your help again on Saturday. I'll pay you well if you're a good helper.''

Jeff looked at Maura for permission. She nodded.

"Okay," her son said, then took the offered money and went off with his sister in tow toward the change machine.

Maura and Wyatt found a booth and sat down across from each other. The high-backed seats and the hanging lamp that threw off dim light made the small space seem more intimate. She immediately felt Wyatt's formidable presence, along with his warmth, and the light scent of his aftershave wafted toward her. The man might be large, but there was a gentleness about him that didn't threaten her.

Maura's thoughts turned to her past, knowing too well how fast things could change. How tenderness could turn into accusing words, caresses into slaps and a swinging fist. She quickly shook off the bad memories of her life with Darren.

"You okay?" Wyatt's voice drew her attention.

Maura released a long breath. "Yes," she said, knowing she was no longer the same woman who'd let herself be controlled, abused. She could protect herself now and that's what she planned to do. Her eyes locked with Wyatt's mesmerizing blue ones.

He was making it difficult not to wish for things she could never have. That didn't stop her curiosity about the man. She had questions. Questions she shouldn't ask, but she couldn't help herself.

"Why did you buy the old Randell ranch?" she blurted out.

Wyatt couldn't fault Maura for her curiosity. If things were reversed, he'd be asking, too.

"I didn't start out to buy it," he said honestly. "I'd only planned to come to San Angelo and talk with Jared Trager. All my life it seems I've been looking for this missing part of me, wondering about the man who fathered me. My mother always refused to tell Dylan or me who he was. Then out of the blue, I got Jared's letter, and she had no choice but tell us about Jack Randell."

"What did she think about you coming here…looking for your father?"

Wyatt glanced toward the video game machines to make sure Jeff was helping his sister. "She wasn't crazy about the idea. Neither was Dylan. My stepfather even less." He raked his fingers through his hair. "I'm the one who needed to confront the man, ask him why he ran off from his responsibilities. Then I got here and discovered that he'd been gone for years. But I was curious about his life…his family."

"That's when you decided to buy the family ranch?"

"I never planned to buy *that* particular ranch," he said truthfully. "When I drove by and saw the For Sale sign, I only went to inquire about the property. Somehow, I ended up offering a ridiculously low price. They accepted it.

"Then that night I came in and found you and the kids at the house, and Cade appeared. How could I say…hey, I'm your long-lost, bastard brother?" Wyatt had known the word too well. He'd lived with it all his life.

Maura saw the pain in Wyatt's eyes and her heart went out to him. As much as she tried to stay uninvolved, it was too late the minute she walked away from the barbecue and climbed into his truck.

Their order number was called and Wyatt went up to get the pizza while she gathered her kids. Kelly sat next to her and she put Jeff beside Wyatt. If her son had a problem, he never voiced it. His only interest was the food.

Maura picked pepperoni off of Kelly's piece and handed it to her. Her daughter smiled. "Thanks, Wyatt, for taking us here. It's fun."

"You're welcome, princess." Wyatt turned to Jeff. "Thanks for watching your sister."

Shyly Jeff said thank you, too.

Maura was happy to see her son coming around. "What are you going to be working on tomorrow?"

"I'm going to be tearing the roof off the porch before it falls down." He glanced at Jeff. "You think you can handle loading the wheelbarrow with the old shingles? Then this weekend I'll be ready to finish nailing the porch floorboards. Maybe you can help me."

Jeff perked up. "Okay," he said, then quickly concentrated on his pizza.

Wyatt glanced across the table. "I'll be right with him all the time. I'd never do anything to put him in jeopardy."

A mother always had fears about her children getting hurt, but her son needed a positive male role model. "If you're sure he won't get in your way."

"Mom, I'm not a baby." Jeff glanced at his sister, but didn't say anything.

"No, he won't get in my way. We'll be fine," Wyatt assured her.

"I know," Maura said. But she had more than her son's physical safety to worry about. It seemed as if Jeff and Kelly were getting far too attached to Wyatt Gentry. She looked at him and her eyes locked with his. A warm sensation poured through her, making her feel things she hadn't felt in a long time.

No, it wasn't just the kids she had to worry about.

The next morning, Hank Barrett drove his truck off the highway onto the gravel road. He passed under the broken gate sign that used to read the Rocking R Ranch. He knew the place well. It was where he'd come to get Chance, Cade and Travis. Every time the young boys ran away from the Circle B, they'd end up back at their old home.

Years ago, most everyone had told him he'd be crazy to take in three hoodlums. And with that bad Randell blood, to boot. Their daddy was a low-down cattle rustler. In west Texas, there wasn't much worse than that.

But Hank knew the young boys needed him. Although they didn't want to come live at the Circle B, the courts had insisted. At fourteen, Chance was too young to look after his brothers. Children's Services had tried to separate them, but somehow they always found a way to get back together. Hank had been the only person who'd take all three of them.

He smiled. "A widowed man without a child of his own... I was doggone crazy."

Although he was lucky enough to discover his daughter, Josie, as far as he was concerned, Chance, Cade and Travis were his sons. He never regretted a day he'd had with the boys.

Now their lives had been rocked again by another of their daddy's transgressions. A second illegitimate son had surfaced—with his twin to come. The rumors in the community were bound to start up again. Not that Hank was worried. His boys were made of tough stuff. They could share their lives with another brother. They'd already come to accept Jared, included him in the family. They would come around again.

Hank stopped in front of the old house. First thing he saw was Wyatt Gentry busy tearing off old shingles from the sagging porch. Hank climbed out of his truck and went up the walk.

Without stopping his task, Gentry spoke, "If you're here to run me off, you're wasting your time." More shingles came flying to the ground.

Hank grinned. There was no doubt this man had Randell blood in his veins. "Can't a neighbor come pay a visit?"

This time Wyatt stopped and glared down at Hank. "You weren't very neighborly last night."

"And you weren't very honest," Hank countered.

They both stared at each other. Finally Wyatt spoke. "Would you like some iced tea?"

"Wouldn't turn it down," Hank said.

Wyatt climbed down the ladder. "Come inside to the kitchen." He held open the screen door and Hank walked in ahead of him. He glanced around the familiar living room. Not much had changed over the years. It needed a lot of work.

"This is a great house. It's a shame that it was neglected over the years."

"You knew Jack Randell?"

"I knew his daddy, John Randell, Sr. His family used to have quite a spread here. A real showplace. After John's death, Jack wasn't any good at running things. He married a local girl, Alice Howard. No sooner had the newlyweds settled in, Jack took off on the rodeo circuit. He was never home and the ranch suffered. When the boy's mother got sick and died, Jack finally came back. He was lousy at managing the ranch—and worse at being a father to three small boys." Hank looked at Wyatt. "I think you already know that he was sent to prison."

Wyatt nodded and started for the kitchen. He pulled two glasses from the cupboard and filled them with tea from a pitcher in the old refrigerator. They both pulled out chairs and sat down.

"Why did you buy this place?"

"Because I've been looking for a ranch, and it was dirt cheap." Wyatt quoted the price.

"Damn! You're right," Hank said. "Ben Roscoe was giving it away."

"I heard it's been on the market for years."

Hank nodded. "Cattle ranching hasn't been that profitable lately. That's the reason we thought it would be a good idea for Maura and the kids to move in here temporarily. We were all shocked when we heard you bought the place. Thanks for letting her stay while she looks for another house."

"That's not a problem."

Hank shook his head. "She sure did do a lot of work here. Needs some paint, but it's clean as a whistle."

Wyatt finished his tea, wondering where Hank Barrett was headed with his inquiries. "Well, I think my break is over and I need to get back to work." He stood and Hank followed him and placed his empty glass in the sink.

"C'mon, I'll help," the older man started through the house. "C'mon..."

"You don't have to..."

Hank stopped. "If I help, I figure it'll take us about an hour to finish, then we can take a ride out to Mustang Valley."

Wyatt had heard about the valley and grinned. "Sounds good."

"Well, let's get crackin', boy. The day's not going to get any cooler." The older man had his sleeves rolled up by the time they reached the porch. He glanced up and eyed the rotted wood. "Besides making it livable, what are your plans for the place?"

"I'll be boarding rodeo rough stock."

Hank grinned. "Well, that's interesting." He looked thoughtful for a minute. "Gentry. Say, your brother wouldn't be 'Devil Dylan' Gentry, the champion bull rider?"

Wyatt smiled proudly. "That's Dylan."

"Well, I'll be damned. Hey, you two wouldn't want to attend my rodeo coming up in at the end of the month? I put it on every year after roundup. All the neighbors are invited."

Hearing the word neighbors, Wyatt's hopes soared. Maybe he did belong here after all.

Maura drove the golf cart down the path to the honeymoon suite. The most secluded cabin of them all, and the most popular one. In the middle of the grove of oak trees a small creek ran just outside the cabin window. On the porch a small table was decorated with two place settings and in a few hours a nice supper would be sent down for this evening's meal. She was here now to deliver the flowers and make sure everything was ready.

She went to the back of her cart and took out the two white-and-green bouquets, one a centerpiece for the table and the other a vase for inside the cabin.

She had an hour to add the finishing touches before the honeymoon couple arrived. After unlocking the door, she walked inside the large room. The flagstone fireplace was filled with kindling, ready for a romantic fire. The overstuffed love seat and matching chairs were nearly covered with fat pillows. Partially covering the planked wood floors was an off-white shag rug that was so thick she was tempted to walk barefoot through the thick pile.

Instead, she went to the small alcove where a deep-red silk comforter covered the large canopy bed. A dozen pillows were arranged against the high, carved-wooden headboard. Numerous candles were arranged around the room.

Maura approached the bed and touched the smooth material, knowing that underneath the covers were ivory satin sheets. She wondered how the cool fabric would feel against her bare skin.

She closed her eyes and pictured herself on the bed. Surprisingly the image of a man appeared. Wyatt. He was naked to the waist, wearing only jeans. She couldn't take her gaze off him, his broad shoulders, his well-defined chest. Her breathing grew labored as he started toward her, his eyes never leaving hers. Standing in front of her, he lowered his head, his mouth so close his warm breath caressed her face. Her body grew warm and achy as her lips parted in anticipation of his kiss.

"Maura," he whispered her name.

"Oh, Wyatt," she said and reached out for him.

"Maura…Maura."

Snapping back from the wonderful reverie, she opened her eyes and gasped when she saw Wyatt standing across the room. He was fully dressed and looking confused.

"Oh—Wyatt." She straightened, she glanced away. "What are you doing here?"

Wyatt was wondering the same thing. But seeing

Maura standing in this room surrounded by flowers and candlelight, he couldn't stop the daydream. Maura lying in bed waiting for her lover...for him. Desire shot through him like hot lava. Hearing his name again, he quickly reined it in.

He pulled off his hat. "I went riding with Hank Barrett. He was showing me around the valley...and I saw you come in here. I thought I'd come by and say hello." He was stumbling over his words like a teenage boy and he noticed her flushed face. "Are you all right?"

She turned away. "I'm fine. Just busy trying to get ready for the ranch's guests."

Wyatt's focus turned to the huge canopy bed and his imagination started off again. He quickly yanked his thoughts back. "So, this is the bridal suite."

"Yes. Lovely isn't it?"

Suddenly soft music came on, the lights dimmed. Oh, boy, this was all he needed. "Hey, this can really set a mood," he tried to joke. "Not that newlyweds need any help," he quipped, wondering why he didn't just shut up.

"It's nice to be romantic," Maura said as she crossed the room and began to arrange the flowers in the vase.

"Your flowers are beautiful. You did a wonderful job arranging the bouquet."

"Thank you. I like to use white, especially on the couples' first night. White stands for unity, love, respect and purity."

He found himself drawn closer, inhaling the fragrance of both the roses and her. To him, Maura's scent was more intoxicating.

"What about red roses? For passion and desire. Wouldn't a bride want her husband to feel those things, too?"

Wyatt watched excitement light her large eyes, then suddenly it faded away. That was when he knew that Maura Wells had never experienced any of the those wonderful emotions.

Deep down, he wished he could be the man to show her what she'd missed.

Chapter Five

After his ride with Hank through the valley, Wyatt returned to the house to finish the job of tearing away the old porch. Hard physical work should help drive away the picture of Maura in the bridal suite from his mind.

With a shake of his head he took the sledgehammer to the railing and began swinging at the rotted wood. The ancient lumber splintered and finally gave way in surrender. Within minutes he'd collapsed the entire section.

"You're a fast worker."

Wyatt turned to find Jared Trager standing in the walkway. The man looked like the rest of the Randells, tall and broad with dark hair. They all had the same easy smile, and a bit of an attitude, as if they didn't give a damn as to what people thought of them.

"Need some help?" he asked.

"I'm doing just fine on my own."

That brought another smile from Trager. "I had the same idea when I came here. I could do everything on my own. Didn't need anyone's help, especially a Randell. It took a while, but I was proven wrong.''

Wyatt kept on working, but Jared wouldn't be ignored. ''You need to give them some time. I don't think you would be here if you didn't want the same thing I wanted. To be accepted.''

''All I wanted was to find out who my father was,'' Wyatt said, his voice strained as he grabbed one end of the railing and began to drag it toward the pile of scrap wood. ''I've done that and I didn't like what I discovered. End of story. I'll survive…and move on.''

Jared took hold of the other end of the railing and helped with the taxing load. ''That's why you bought this place? So you could move on? There has to be dozens of ranches like this around the country, including Arizona.'' They dropped the section of porch on top of the pile with a grunt. Jared raised his hands. ''I know…the price was right, but I think you wanted more when you decided to come here. I think you wanted a sense of family. A place to belong, like I said.'' His eyes held Wyatt's. ''I was looking for the same thing when I showed up at the Lazy S and found Dana and Evan.''

''Our stories are totally different,'' Wyatt insisted, then turned and headed back to what was left of the porch.

''Maybe, but not by much. A man named Jack Randell fathered us all, and he didn't give a damn. In spite of that, we seemed to have turned out to be decent guys. And in spite of everything else, that's a bond between all of us. Chance, Cade, Travis, you, Dylan and me. We're brothers.''

Wyatt felt a tug on his heart at hearing those words, but he tried not to show any emotion. He still had a lot to work through.

"It's going to take a while," Jared continued. "I even went through DNA testing to prove that I was a Randell. At least your mother verified Jack was your father."

"Doesn't make any difference," Wyatt said. "The Randells don't want me here."

"Give 'em a chance." Jared frowned, reminding Wyatt so much of Dylan. "It's hard for Chance, Cade and Travis to keep hearing about their father's transgressions." Jared raked his hand through his hair. "I should have been here when you arrived, if only to prepare them."

Wyatt wasn't in the mood to talk anymore. He wasn't about to beg the Randells for acceptance, either. "Doesn't make any difference now. I'm here and like it or not, I'm stayin'."

That made Jared grin. "Good. Let me know if you want any help putting the new porch on. I need to get home to supper. I have a pregnant wife who can't think about anything but food right now."

Jared started toward his black truck and Wyatt found himself calling out to him. "Saturday. I'll be working on the porch frame."

He saluted. "I'll be here as soon as I finish the morning chores. Say around eight?"

"Thanks," Wyatt called out.

"No problem. That's what family is for." Jared climbed in his truck and started off just as Maura's station wagon came up the road. She parked and the kids jumped out. They both came running toward him, Kelly stumbling and nearly falling in her excitement. Jeff made it first, but his sister was quickly at his side. Wyatt found his mood brightening, especially since Jeff had been more accepting of him.

"Hi, Wyatt," the girl said with a big smile.

"Hello, princess. How was your day?"

"We went to the library. I got books, but I can't keep them, I have to give them back. So I hafta be careful. You want to see?" She pulled them out of her backpack.

"Sure." He leaned down and examined her books, one about a lost kitten and the other a velveteen rabbit. He glanced at Jeff. The boy was dying to talk but didn't want to appear anxious.

"How was your day, Jeff?"

He shrugged. "We practiced for a fire drill and I learned how not to burn up in a fire."

"You don't say. How is that?"

The boy proceeded to drop down and roll on the ground. Maura came up the walk. "Jeffrey Wells, what are you doing in your good school clothes?"

"Uh-oh," the boy echoed.

"Sorry, Maura," Wyatt said. "It was my fault. I was just asking what they did in school today. Jeff was showing me how to stop, drop and roll in a fire."

Maura's heart rate accelerated. One look at the man, even dirty and sweaty from work, and she couldn't find her voice. Same as when he'd first come to the cabin. She could never go into the bridal suite again and not picture him there.

She pulled her gaze away and looked at her children. "Okay, you both go upstairs and change your clothes. Dinner will be ready soon." She started off and he stopped her.

"Can I vote for hamburgers?" Wyatt asked while the kids cheered. "I happened to buy a grill today and I was wondering if we could try it out and cook some burgers."

"Oh, can we, Mom?" Kelly pleaded.

Maura didn't like to have to disappoint them. "Not tonight, kids. I don't have any ground beef."

"I also stopped at the grocery store and got some meat and buns."

Maura didn't know what to say. The man was taking over her one job—fixing his meals. She sent the kids into the house.

"Look, Wyatt. How am I supposed to fulfill my part of our agreement if you keep paying for the food?"

"If you're talking about the pizza last night, it was my fault you and the kids missed supper. And as for tonight, it's been so hot lately, I thought cooking outside would keep the house cooler."

She crossed her arms. "I won't take charity, Wyatt."

"Okay." He reached into his pocket, pulled out the grocery receipt and handed it to her. "I bought a few other things that I needed, but the cost of the meat and buns are on there. You can pay me back."

She nodded, knowing maybe she was a little over the line, but she wasn't going to be dependant on a man again. It would be so easy to rely on someone like Wyatt Gentry. He was big and strong, yet gentle and caring. She could see that every time he was with her and Jeff and Kelly. And darn it, her own pulse raced whenever he came close. But she wasn't a foolish girl any more. A sweet talking man couldn't sway her. Her breath quickened. No matter how handsome he was.

She took out her wallet, counted out the four dollars for the food and handed it to him. "Please try to understand, Wyatt. I need to pay my own way."

He nodded. "I understand. In fact, you remind me a lot of my mother. She taught her boys the same. Do an honest day's work for an honest day's pay."

Maura glanced around. "Looks like you've done more than your share today."

"The tear down is the easy part. It's cleaning up and rebuilding that's going to take the time."

"Well, don't let Jeff get in your way. I'm not sure how much of a help he'll be."

"Let me worry about him."

"Thank you for taking time with him," she said. "He hasn't had much experience with a positive role model."

"Whoa, don't make me out to be something I'm not. I just want to help the boy lose a little attitude."

She found herself smiling at his embarrassment. "Whatever, I thank you. I think I'll make some potato salad and deviled eggs. We'll make it a picnic."

He shook his head. "The way you've been feeding me, I think I better worry about my waistline."

Her gaze went to his trim waist and flat stomach. She wondered what it'd be like to open the buttons on his shirt, to run her fingers over his sweat slick skin, his taut muscles and broad shoulders. Realizing what she was doing, her gaze moved to his face. "You don't have anything to worry about."

But she sure did if she didn't stop having these wanton thoughts.

Saturday morning arrived and so did Jared. Without much discussion, the two went to work and built the frame for the new porch. Somewhere around nine o'clock, Maura came out with some iced tea for them and lemonade for Jeff, who'd been working on picking up the scraps of wood. They all sat down for a well-deserved break.

"Looks like we're making some headway," Jared said. "I'll help you finish this, but I need to be home by noon. Evan has a soccer game and I help coach the team.'' He nodded at Jeff as he went back to work at the edge of the yard. ''I tried to talk the boy into playing, but he didn't seem interested.'' Jared shook his head. ''It's tough being the new kid in school. I don't think he's made many friends, yet.''

''I know how that feels,'' Wyatt offered. ''With all the traveling we did as kids, our mom had to do a lot of the schooling herself. We weren't around much to make many friends. Maura said Jeff misses Dallas.''

''Maybe Jeff will be ready for baseball in the spring.'' Jared took the last swallow of his tea. ''That is, if they stay here.''

Wyatt was surprised to hear that Maura was thinking about leaving San Angelo. ''I didn't know she was leaving the area.''

''She only planned to stay temporarily. Just to get away from her ex-husband.'' Jared frowned. ''I shouldn't have said anything.''

''It's okay. I know she has an ex out there.'' Wyatt thought back to the promise he'd made that he'd do whatever it took to protect her and her kids if the man ever showed up and caused trouble.

''She has a good job at the Yellow Rose, but it costs a lot to support herself and two kids.'' Jared gave him a sideways glance. ''You've been good to let her stay here.''

Wyatt told himself not to think about trying to help her, not to get involved any more than he already was. She and the kids weren't his problem, but he couldn't keep himself from asking, ''I take it her ex wasn't a nice guy?''

Jared stiffened. ''Don't know him, but from what I gather, the guy's a jerk. The scum had a way with his fists. Luckily, Maura got away. I think she's still afraid that he'll find her and the kids.'' Jared looked at him. ''Again, it's great that you let them stay.''

''No big deal. I hadn't planned on moving into the house at first anyway. I still have a lot of work to do. Speaking of which, we need to get back to it. It's not getting any cooler.'' He stood and grabbed his hammer.

In another hour the porch frame was finished and Jared headed home. Tomorrow, Wyatt planned to hang the shingles. The new railing had been milled and assembled at the local lumberyard, and was being delivered on Monday. He needed to have everything ready. That meant the porch floor had to be finished this weekend. He turned to the six-year-old working in the yard. ''Hey, Jeff, you think you can help me hammer a few nails?''

His eyes rounded. ''I never used a hammer before.''

''Well, come up here and I'll show you.''

The boy had worked like the devil all morning. To Wyatt's surprise he never complained once. He hesitated to ask him for more. Maybe he should send Jeff inside to rest, but he didn't want to disappoint him if he wanted to stay.

Thirty minutes later, Maura helped when she called them inside for lunch. After washing up, Wyatt sat down at the kitchen table to two egg salad sandwiches and leftover potato salad. The kids ate peanut-butter sandwiches.

''You didn't have to make me special sandwiches,'' he told Maura. ''I like peanut butter.'' He winked at Kelly.

The girl giggled as she ate around the bread crust.

Maura came to the table. ''You don't like egg salad?''

''Yes, I like egg salad very much,'' he stressed. ''Just

don't go to so much trouble for me. I'm sure you have plenty else to do.''

''It's fine,'' she said. ''That reminds me, I washed your clothes and took the basket down to the cottage.''

''There was no need to,'' he said, recalling the condition of the cottage. ''I could have taken it down myself.''

He watched as Maura moved around the kitchen. She had her hair tied up in a ponytail, but nearly half the silky strands were curled around her face. She wore a pair of shorts, showing off trim calves and shapely thighs. A large white T-shirt was knotted at her tiny waist.

''You've been busy,'' she said. ''Besides, it's part of our agreement.''

Wyatt was starting to hate their agreement. He found he looked forward to her coming home every day, hearing about the kids' day at school. It seemed so natural, all of them being here. But truth was, she would be gone one day…and soon. He had to accept that.

By the next week, Wyatt had nearly completed the repairs to the house. He had finished rebuilding the porches, both front and back. Most of the peeling paint had been scraped off. Now, he was busy replacing the cracked windows and puttying the ones that were still intact.

The late September morning was another hot one. Wyatt chose to spend it on a twenty-foot ladder to work on the second story, finishing the last row of windows. Next he would prime and paint. He already bought twenty-five gallons of oil base, whisper-white for the house and forest-green for the shutters.

He smiled in amazement as he spread putty along the

pane. It had been three weeks since he'd taken possession of the property. Well, maybe not exactly possession, since he shared the place with a woman and her kids. But he wouldn't have changed the last few weeks for anything.

In fact, he was going to miss Maura's special touches, and not just in the house. She'd managed to weave some hominess into the cottage, finding time to clean and organize his temporary living quarters. No use in trying to stop her, she would just insist she was paying her way. Fine. He wasn't about to argue with a stubborn female.

Correction. A beautiful, stubborn female that he was going to miss a lot.

Wyatt was just scrapping the last pane when he reached for his knife and began to slip on the ladder rung. Losing his balance, he grabbed at the window but couldn't get a good grip. With no time to think, he pushed himself away, praying he'd land on the ground and not atop the ladder. Wyatt got his wish and tumbled to the hard ground with a thud. Pain sliced through his body, especially his back and legs as every bit of air was forced from his lungs. His last thoughts were of Maura and the kids. He hated the thought of her finding him like this.

Then everything went black.

Maura returned to the house to pick up Jeff's permission slip for the field trip so she could fax it to the school. Inside the house, she found the paper on the table, right where her son had left it. She started to leave, but decided to let Wyatt know she stopped by.

She'd been surprised that she hadn't seen him. Going on a search, she went out through the kitchen and called out his name. No answer. She then walked around back and froze seeing him sprawled on the ground.

"Wyatt!" She raced to his side and she knelt down beside his motionless body. "Oh, God. Please, let him be all right," she whispered, tears already filling her eyes. She felt for his pulse and found one, then she heard him groan. "Wyatt, I'm here. Don't move."

"I don't think I can." He groaned again. "I hurt," he managed and opened his eyes when she touched his face.

"I'll take care of you." She continued to stroke his face, then realized she had to get him help. "Wyatt, I've got to go call someone, but I'll be right back."

Swallowing back her panic, Maura ran to the house. First she called for an ambulance, then Cade. He told her he'd meet her at the hospital. After hanging up, she got a blanket and a cup of ice and hurried outside.

"I'm back, Wyatt," she said, and sank down beside him.

He blinked at her, then opened those gorgeous blue eyes. This time he smiled. "I guess I zigged instead of zagged," he joked, but pain was etched on his face.

Maura saw the extension ladder laying on the ground and knew he had been working on the second story. She closed her eyes. He could have been killed, he could have a spinal injury. She sent up a silent prayer. *Please, don't let anything happen to him.*

"Here's some ice," she offered, not knowing how long he'd been lying there. Luckily he'd been in the shady side of the house. She placed an ice sliver against his lips and he drew it into his mouth.

"Where do you hurt?"

"Everywhere." His breathing was labored. "That's good. At least I can feel every part of my body."

"You shouldn't have been up there without someone to hold the ladder."

"You sound like my mother."

"Well, I am *a* mother. And when you do foolish things…" Tears flooded her eyes and ran down her face. "Darn it, Wyatt, you may have really hurt yourself."

He glanced up at her, then raised his hand to her eyes and touched a tear. "Don't cry, Maura, I'm fine. I've been hurt worse in my rodeoing days when I got tossed off broncs."

She didn't believe him. "Do you want me to call someone? Your family?"

He took her hand and gripped tight. "No. You're all I need."

She brushed away another tear. "Oh, Wyatt. I'm not sure what I can do for you."

"You're doin' fine…"

Maura touched his hair and brushed it back. She couldn't deny that this man had come to mean so much to her. More than she ever wanted to admit. She prayed that he would be all right.

He hated hospitals.

Wyatt lay on the cold metal exam table, his back hurting like hell as he waited for the doctor. Maura was outside, probably pacing. He knew he'd scared her. The look on her face, and the panic in her voice had told him that. Hell, he'd scared himself.

The pain in his back was so bad he was sweating by the time Maura had reached him. But he soon forgot the discomfort the second she put her hands on him. Her touch, her soothing voice… Maybe she revealed more than she wanted, but she cared about him.

Just then a young doctor walked in. "Well, Mr. Gentry, you didn't break anything, but it seems you twisted your ankle and have a bad back sprain." He smiled as he glanced up from the chart. "All in all, I'd say you were a lucky guy."

"Good, then I can go home."

The doctor raised his hand. "Just let me explain a few things about your care, first. I better get your wife in here. She's been so worried."

Before Wyatt could say anything to the doctor, he ushered Maura into the room. "Mrs. Gentry, I was just about to tell your husband that if he wants to go home, he'll need complete bed rest for the next five to seven days."

Wyatt could see Maura's blush at the doctor's assumption, but neither one of them said a word as the doctor reeled off his instructions.

"Wyatt, your back isn't going to heal overnight. You're going to be in pain for a while." He began writing on the chart. "So I'm prescribing some painkillers."

"I don't need any pills."

Maura looked at Wyatt sternly, then spoke, "Doctor, I'll make sure *my husband* follows your instructions, even if I have to tie him up."

With a groan Wyatt laid back on the table, trying not to think about the different kind of pain Maura was going to inflict on him.

Wyatt was actually relieved when Cade showed up to help him get home. All he needed was bed rest for the day, and he'd feel better tomorrow. Maura climbed in the back seat and they drove by the pharmacy to get the pills. When they'd reached the ranch, they helped Wyatt into the house.

"Where are you taking me?" he demanded weakly.

"Upstairs into the master bedroom," Maura said to Cade, who had Wyatt's arm over his shoulders, helping him navigate the stairs. By the time they reached the large room, Wyatt felt like he'd run a mile. He was breathing hard and unable to argue about what room they deposited him in.

Maura had pulled back the comforter and blanket, exposing flowery sheets. No doubt this was her bedroom.

"Maura, I can't take your room."

She ignored him. "I'm going downstairs to make some lunch. Cade, will you help Wyatt undress?"

As Cade nodded, she disappeared from the room.

"I'm not staying here," Wyatt insisted.

"Why not? It's your house."

"I can't take Maura's bed."

"Then you're going to have to leave under your own power," Cade challenged. "But if you know what's good for you, you'll just stop fighting and take the time to heal. From what I hear, you came pretty close to doing some real damage to yourself."

Wyatt ignored Cade as he tried to pull his shirt from the waistband of his jeans. He had zero strength. Without a word, Cade took over and did the job for him.

Once his boots and jeans were removed, Wyatt wasn't feeling good at all. His back was going into spasms. He grimaced as Cade helped him under the sheets.

Maura returned with soup and a pitcher of ice water. Without a word, she took out a pill and handed it to him.

Wyatt didn't hesitate. He wanted relief from the pain. He tossed the small pill into his mouth, then drank the entire glass of water.

The last thing he remembered were the soft sounds of Maura's voice and her touch, then he was oblivious to anything after that.

* * *

"How are you going to handle this on your own?" Abby asked from across the kitchen table. Maura's friend had come by with supper for her and the kids, then helped clean up.

"There's not much to handle. Wyatt's in bed."

"But what happens when he needs to get out of bed…when he needs to go to the bathroom? You want Cade to spend the night?"

Maura shook her head. "That's the reason I put him in my room. The bathroom is close. I can get him there. Cade has been wonderful. And both he and Jared promised to stop by tomorrow."

Abby nodded. "Okay, but don't worry about the Yellow Rose. Your new assistant, Carol, can run the shop for a few days. Luckily there isn't anything special coming up until next weekend." She stood up. "Just call if you need anything."

Maura nodded. "And Abby, thank you for giving me the time off," she said walking her friend to the door.

"Are you kidding? It's you who's brought in the business. Your arrangements are unique, Maura. Do you know we had two orders for bouquets today and both customers insisted that you do the arrangements?"

Maura was pleased, but surprised. "I could come in tomorrow for a few hours when Jared comes by."

Abby raised her hand. "Not necessary. Luckily they're both for this next weekend. The only thing I need you to do is order the flowers from the wholesale mart." A big smile appeared. "Isn't it wonderful? We're suddenly in demand."

Maura was excited, too, but she couldn't think of anything other than helping Wyatt recover. "It's nice to know we're wanted," Maura said as she walked Abby out.

She waved as the car drove off. Thank God things had quieted down. She was grateful that some of the Randell family had wanted to help, but it felt as if nearly every one of them had stopped by, dropping off food, offering to help out. And Wyatt had slept through all the commotion. Just as well. He needed sleep more than anything else.

Maura locked the doors and shut off the lights before she climbed the stairs. She found Jeff in his room. Her son had bathed and dressed in pajamas without even being told.

She went to him, took him in her arms and kissed his cheek.

"Thanks for helping out today."

He nodded. "Mom, is Wyatt going to be okay?"

She could see the fear in her son's eyes. "Sure, he's going to be fine," she assured him. "His back will be really sore for about a week." She brushed her son's hair away from his face, tickled that he hadn't pulled away from her. "And I have to thank you, Jeff. I had to come home to get your permission slip, or Wyatt wouldn't have been found for a long time."

He smiled. "Then I'm glad I missed the dumb trip. And I'm glad Wyatt is okay."

"I'm sure he'd like to hear that."

"And tomorrow after school, I'm going to finish cleaning up the yard."

She hugged him again, then walked out of the room. Next, she went looking for her daughter. Not surprising, Kelly's bedroom was empty. Maura walked down the hall to her room. She heard Kelly's tiny voice even before she went inside. Wyatt was stretched out under the covers and Kelly was seated next to him. Her library book was open and she was pretending to read the words as she made up her own.

"And they lived happily ever after...forever and ever. The end," she said and closed the book. "You want me to read it again?"

A groggy Wyatt could barely speak. "Not tonight, princess."

Maura decided to rescue him. "It's time for this princess to go to bed," she announced as she crossed the room. "And Wyatt needs his sleep, too."

Kelly bent down and carefully kissed his rough cheek. "I'm glad you're feelin' better. Good night, Wyatt."

Maura looked at Wyatt. "I'll be right back," she promised, then took Kelly off to her room. She tucked her in for the night, promising her daughter she'd be right back to share her bed.

Maura returned to Wyatt's room to find him struggling to get up. She rushed to his side. "Whoa, you can't get out of bed."

He was shirtless and a pair of black sweats rode low on his slim hips. His hair was practically standing on end and he needed a shave. He was more appealing than ever. "I better or I'm going to embarrass myself. And I haven't had an accident in bed since I was four years old." He grimaced. "If I have to, I'll crawl to the toilet."

"How about if I help you?" She braced her feet on the floor and held out her hands. "Grab hold and I'll pull you up."

He looked unconvinced that she could get him to his feet.

"I'm stronger than I look." She gripped his hands and after a few tries she had him standing. "See, I told you." She moved to his side and placed his arm over her shoulders. "Now, slow, easy steps." They finally made it to the door.

"This is as far as you go," he said, reaching for the door frame.

She found herself blushing. "I'll wait here."

He murmured something she didn't want to decipher. After a few minutes, she heard a flush and water running, then the door opened.

Wyatt had to bite his lip, anything to try to mask his pain. He didn't want Maura to worry anymore. She needed her rest tonight. She'd already spent too much time caring for him. Not that he didn't like it, but she had too much on her plate as it was.

He was weak, but determined not to show it. She came up beside him and placed her arm around his waist.

"Lean on me."

"As if I have a choice," he groaned, feeling her delicate body against his. Damn, the pills sure didn't slow down his libido. He felt every curve and smelled her wonderful scent, making him more light-headed than any drug.

Once he was back down, she took out two more tablets and handed them to him. He took them along with a glass of water.

"Oh, that tastes good. Cooling."

Maura poured him another, then went to the windows and made sure they were opened. Though a slight breeze was coming in, it was still warm in the room. "I could bring in the fan," she offered, then went to the closet and took out a table fan. She plugged it in and immediately the air started cooling off the stifling room. "How is that?"

"Good…"

She then began to straighten the sheets.

"Maura, stop," he insisted, his mouth suddenly dry, his tongue fuzzy. The pills were working. "I'm fine."

She leaned over him to arrange his pillow. Damn, she was killing him. "Are you in a comfortable position? You want me to help…"

He shook his head.

She finally turned off the bedside light. The moonlight through the window illuminated the room enough so he could still see her. He looked up and discovered their faces were mere inches apart. Unable to resist, he raised his hand and took hold of her wrist. "Did I thank you for taking care of me?"

She nodded. "Yes, many times," she whispered, her warm breath teasing his cheek.

"Maura…you are so beautiful." He drew her hand to his face, then turned and kissed the warm palm. She gasped but didn't pull away, nor did she fight him when he reached out and drew her head down to his.

He knew this was crazy, but couldn't stop himself. For days he'd ached to kiss her… The touch of her lips was like a spark that ignited a blaze. She whimpered and he took another nibble, then another, until he grew hungry for more. And she gave it to him. He cupped the back of her head and feasted on her delicious mouth.

He was in agony, but it wasn't in his back.

Chapter Six

What was she doing?

Maura suddenly came to her senses and tore her mouth from his. Seeing the desirous look in Wyatt's eyes, she gasped and quickly stepped back from the bed.

"I have to go," she whispered, then hurried from the room.

Once inside Kelly's room, she shut the door and sank against it, trying to draw a breath. She touched her lips, still able to feel his firm mouth...his intoxicating taste. Her heart raced, not from fear or regret, but surprisingly from desire.

The experience was nothing like when Darren had come after her. Drunk and demanding, he'd taken what he wanted, leaving her... Maura closed her eyes to shut out the pain of her ex-husband's abuse and Wyatt's face appeared, along with the soothing feel of his roughened hands against her skin. She had never known that being with a man could feel like that.

Abby had told Maura how tender Cade was with her,

and promised that some day she would find a man who would love her that way. At the time, Maura hadn't wanted to think about being with any man.

That was before Wyatt.

Maura walked to the bed, her body still tingling from his kiss. She scooted her daughter over slightly and climbed in the double bed, then pulled the sheet over both of them. As much as she longed for someone in her life, she couldn't let it go any further. She had her children to think about…and there was Darren. He wanted revenge and he would come after her, ruining any chance she would have for happiness.

She couldn't allow anyone to get hurt because of her, especially a man who had been nothing but kind to her and her kids. She closed her eyes, reliving Wyatt's kiss, knowing that was all she would ever have.

A memory.

A house had fallen on him, Wyatt was sure of it as the early morning sunlight came through the window and woke him. He attempted to get up, but collapsed back on the bed when his body refused to cooperate. Still groggy from the leftover effects of the pills and sleep, he finally managed to swing his feet off the bed and sit up. He fisted his hands on the edge of the mattress and tried to stand. Just then the door opened and Maura walked in.

"Wyatt!" She rushed to him and helped him up. "Couldn't you wait for me?"

"There are some things a man's gotta do on his own."

"You do a bad imitation of John Wayne."

He didn't feel like it, but he couldn't help but smile. He needed a pain pill in the worst way, but had to get his wits about him before he spent another day in a fog of drugs. Drugs that made him do crazy things, like kissing Maura. Damn, she had to think he was lower than a snake.

After finishing in the bathroom, he opened the door to find her still there, waiting for him. She was dressed in jeans that hugged her shapely legs and a blouse that tapered in at her tiny waist. His gaze moved to her face. Devoid of makeup, she looked natural and pretty and he liked that. She had yet to look at him with those big brown eyes of hers. He didn't blame her. He'd had no business manhandling her last night. He wanted to blame the drugs, but he'd known exactly what he was doing.

Finally they made it back to the bed. She released him and stepped back. "Do you need anything before I start breakfast?"

"Yes, your forgiveness," he said, then didn't know where to begin. "I was out of line last night, Maura. I had no right to kiss you. I only…meant…to thank you for all your help, but the pills made me a little crazy. I promise you don't have to worry about it happening again."

"It's okay," she said. "Just forget about it. I need to go and get your breakfast."

Maura nearly raced for the door. She didn't want to let Wyatt know what that kiss had meant to her. She was crazy to have thought that he felt the same. The man was good-looking. He could have any woman he wanted. Why would he want to get involved with someone with a hundred problems and two kids, to boot?

She found her way down to the kitchen, angry with herself for ever thinking about the man. She had to put things in perspective. Very soon, she'd be out of here, and Wyatt would be moving on with his life, his business. And someday, he'd marry a beautiful woman who didn't have a past with an ex-husband who was set on getting even.

"Mom, do I have to go to school today?"

Maura turned to find her son still wearing his pajamas. "Of course you do."

"But I need to help Wyatt," he insisted.

"Honey, Wyatt would be the first to tell you how important school is. Besides, Cade and Jared are coming by today to help out." She went to him. "But if you want, you can help when you come home. I'm not going to work today so the bus will drop you off here. After you finish your homework, you can help until suppertime."

Jeff opened his mouth to argue, but instead he smiled. "Okay. I'll do my homework on the bus." He rushed off to get ready for school as Kelly walked into the room already dressed for the day. "I wanna eat breakfast with Wyatt 'cause he's lonely."

"I think Wyatt needs a little quiet time. But I'll let you help me carry up his food. Why don't you go outside and see if you can find some pretty flowers to take him?"

Kelly shot out the door and ran past Cade Randell coming up the back steps. "Good morning," he said to Maura.

"Good morning," she greeted him and offered him a cup of coffee.

"How's the patient?" he asked as he took a seat at the table. "Any problems?"

Just that the man kisses like a dream. She shook her head. "He's quiet now, but earlier I caught him attempting to get out of bed by himself."

"Uh-oh, I was afraid of that. Do you want me to send in the big artillery? I could have Ella over here in thirty minutes."

Maura had heard stories about the Circle B's house-keeper. "In his weakened state, drugged and disabled, I think I can handle him."

Cade smiled and it reminded her of Wyatt.

"You know, I can see a resemblance between the two of you."

His smile faded. "I know I didn't behave real well toward Wyatt when we heard the news. But you have no idea how tired we are hearing about good old Jack's exploits. I have nothing against Wyatt personally, it's just…hearing his news took a little getting used to. Maybe with this accident we'll get the chance to get to know him." He took a drink of coffee.

Maura joined him at the table. "You and your broth-ers are good people. Whatever you do, I know you'll be fair."

He nodded. "We try. I was looking around outside. Jared told me Wyatt was doing a lot of repairs on the place. I had no idea he'd gotten so much done."

"He starts before I leave for the day and is working until the sun goes down," she informed him. "He said he and his brother, Dylan, spent a lot of their lives living out of a trailer and traveling around with the rodeo."

"I take it that was where Jack met their mother."

She shrugged. "I think you and Wyatt should be talk-ing about this." She got up from the table and poured another cup of coffee. "I better get him some breakfast. Here, take this up to him and get to know the man. He's your brother."

Cade took the mug along with his own. "Bossy

woman. You've been hanging around Abby too much. You're beginning to sound just like her.''

Maura smiled. ''I take that as a compliment''

''You should, she's a helluva woman.''

She couldn't help but wonder what it would be like to have a man love her like that. She knew about the history between Abby and Cade and how many long years it took them to find each other again.

Cade stopped in the doorway and looked back at her. ''Since Wyatt's gotten all the prep work on the house finished and there's plenty of paint in the barn, I was thinking that maybe Chance, Travis, Jared and I might have some spare time to start painting the house.''

''Oh, that's a wonderful idea,'' she said. ''But I don't think Wyatt would ask you to do it.''

A big grin appeared. ''If he's drugged for the next few days, I think we might be able to get away without telling him.''

For the next few days while the Randell brothers painted the house, Maura was busy playing nurse to her patient. She figured that Wyatt wasn't going to spend more than three, maybe four days in bed. The doctor ordered five, but the way things were going, she'd be lucky to keep him off his feet until the weekend. He was taking fewer of his pills and becoming more and more aware of things going on.

Maura also needed to go into the flower shop and help Carol fill some orders. Kelly would go with her and spend time at preschool. Since Cade was at the house, he promised to keep an eye on Wyatt.

For three days, the brothers had been working tirelessly on the house. They came over in the morning right after their chores, worked until about noon then returned to their own ranches.

Maura was right. By the fourth day, Wyatt was spending less and less time asleep. Finally he refused to take any more painkillers during the day, only to help him sleep at night. It wouldn't be long before he discovered what was going on.

Wyatt was sick and tired of lying around in bed. In fact, he hated it. His back still hurt, but the pain was tolerable, and he needed to get back on his feet. First on the list was a real shower. He was tired of so-called sponge baths.

He got out of bed and shuffled himself to the bathroom. After closing the door, he brushed aside the plastic shower curtain and turned the water on in the chipped, claw-foot tub, then stripped off his sweat pants. Grabbing the towel rack for support, he slowly raised his leg over the edge and managed to pull himself under the spray of warm water. He just stood there and let the water sluice over his body, invigorating him. He turned so the spray hit his lower back, making him sigh in pleasure. Who would have thought that a shower would have been his biggest turn on in months?

Well, that wasn't exactly true.

Maura Wells had been on his mind far too much. In fact he couldn't get her out of his head. The past few days, she'd missed work to take care of him. Suddenly he realized that as of this Monday she would have been here a month. That had been the agreed upon time limit. She was supposed to move out. How could he let her and the kids leave? She had nowhere to go. Besides, with her nursing duties, how could she have found the time to look for another place?

And why did she have to leave? Their arrangement

wasn't so bad. The kids were happy. He was happy. Who wouldn't be happy to have a beautiful woman around? He'd been afraid that she'd panic when he touched her, but she seemed to trust him. When he kissed her he'd seen the desire in her big brown eyes. He couldn't help but wonder if they darkened when she made love. His body stirred to life.

He groaned and dunked his head under the spray, then grabbed the shampoo and lathered his scalp just as he heard a loud knock on the door.

"Wyatt, are you all right?" Maura called to him.

Beautiful, but maybe a little annoying, too. "I'm fine," he yelled back.

The door cracked opened to the steam filled room. "Cade is here. You want me to get him to help you?"

He cursed under his breath. "I don't need help. Can't a man have some peace?"

There was a long pause, then he heard the door shut.

Damn. He quickly rinsed off, then retrieved a towel from the rack. After drying off, he wrapped it around his waist and carefully climbed out of the tub. He opened the door to find Maura sitting on the edge of the bed. She jumped up, looking strangely guilty and innocent at the same time.

"See, I made it," he said, ignoring the fact that he had on next to nothing. "All by myself."

She didn't say a word, just got up and walked out of the room.

He couldn't stand it and called her back. She stopped at the door.

"What do you want?" she asked.

"I'm sorry," he said. "I should have told you I was going to shower."

"I wouldn't have stopped you, Wyatt. I was just concerned about you getting in and out of that old tub. But I can see you did just fine." Her gaze raked over his body, and he felt the heat searing his skin as if she were touching him. "You're right, you don't need me." With those parting words, she walked out and closed the door.

He let out a breath, then found a fresh pair of sweats in the dresser and pulled them on. It seemed to take him forever and afterward he fell back on the bed exhausted. There was a knock on the door.

Maura was back. He struggled to sit up. "Come in."

Cade peered inside. "Can you handle some company?"

"Sure." He hadn't seen Cade in a few days. "But I warn you, I'm in a hell of a mood."

"Sounds like you're feeling better." Cade walked in and behind him were Jared, Chance and Travis.

"What is this, a party?" he asked.

"Just thought we could talk," Jared said as he and Cade sat in the chairs next to the bed, while Travis and Chance leaned against the dresser.

"You guys here to run me out of town?" Wyatt tried to joke.

"No, we're here to welcome you," Chance said. "As the oldest…" He cocked an eyebrow. "I am the eldest, aren't I?"

"I'm thirty-one," Wyatt stated.

Travis grinned. "Looks like I lost my place as baby of the family. You and your twin, Dylan, have that distinction now."

Wyatt got a strange feeling in his gut when Cade mentioned family. But that was what they were. Family. "My mother always refused to tell us who our father was," he began. "She said it was because she discovered too late that Jack was already married."

Jared began to share his story. "My mother passed away before I ever got a chance to ask her," he added. "I got the news from an old letter of hers. When she learned she was pregnant with me, Jack Randell rebuffed her. She married another man, Graham Hastings. For years, I thought he was my father and never understood why he resented me so much. It wasn't until my brother, Marsh Hastings, died that I learned the truth."

"Maybe you two were lucky," Chance began. "We've been Randells all our lives and have paid a heavy price for our daddy's sins. There are still some people around here who will have nothing to do with us. You might find settling in West Texas wasn't such a great idea."

Wyatt saw the deep pain on Chance's face. "When I came to San Angelo, all I wanted was to know about my roots. To meet Jared. It's strange to suddenly learn you have a family and you have an opportunity to meet them. When I came by this ranch and saw the For Sale sign, I went to a real estate agent just for some information. When he saw my interest in the place, he convinced me to make a bid. I gave him a ridiculously low offer and he took it."

"You got a good deal," Chance said. "If we get rain, this is good grazing land."

"I'm going to keep rough stock," he told them.

Travis grinned and said, "Hey, I hear our brother is the one and only 'Devil Dylan' Gentry. When do we get to meet him?"

Wyatt didn't want to lie to them. "I'm not sure. Dylan's not as excited as I was knowing about his father. I may have to coax him here."

"Damn. I was hoping he'd come for the Circle B

Roundup and Rodeo.'' Travis shrugged. "Oh, well, Hank doesn't have bull riding events anyhow.''

"Dylan and I used to compete in the team calf-roping events. Until he decided that it was too tame to suit him.''

Travis smiled with a faraway look in his eyes. "I bet he gets his share of the girls, too.''

Chance nudged his brother. "Hey, why should you be thinking about such things when you have Josie?''

All the brothers laughed.

"My wife knows I adore her and our daughter, little Alissa Mae,'' Travis insisted.

Wyatt got caught up in the kidding, too. Each one of his brothers was happily married to a beautiful independent women. Despite their childhoods, they all had turned out to be completely unlike their father. Family came first. No doubt Hank Barrett had had a lot of influence on them.

"Speaking of good-looking women,'' Travis began. "What's it like to have your own private nurse?''

"At the moment, I don't think she's talking to me,'' he confessed. "I haven't been in the best mood.''

"I think you better do something about that,'' Cade said. "Never leave a woman to brood for too long. The punishment just gets worse.'' He looked at Wyatt. "If you want your home happy I suggest you try and smooth things over.''

Wyatt was surprised. Were they giving him the okay to pursue Maura?

Wyatt decided to talk with Maura, but she hardly ever stayed in his room long enough to carry on a conversation. He was at fault, but would she ever forgive him? Okay, so he'd been a little grouchy, as Kelly would say.

How could he explain that he'd been dreaming about her, about their kiss…? Not only that, he liked having her around. She had become so much a part of his life.

The kids had, too.

Even Jeff had surprised him. Every day the boy had been cleaning up the wood scraps and sweet little Kelly sat with him in the afternoon reading to him, chatting away about her day. But when Maura came anywhere near him, she refused to say a word that wasn't necessary. He'd hurt her and now he had to try to make her understand.

That night when she came in his room, he was waiting for her.

"Maura, I'd like a word with you."

She paused at the door.

"Think you could come and sit down?" He motioned to the chair beside the bed. "I promise I won't try anything, but we need to clear the air."

She came across the room, but didn't sit down. "If it's about my leaving…"

"Yes, that's one of the subjects I had in mind."

She frowned. "I know it's the end of the month…"

"Yes it is, that's why I wanted to talk—"

"We can be moved out in a few days." She started to leave, when he reached out and grabbed her arm to stop her. She stiffened and he released her, silently cursing her ex for causing her such fear.

"Maura, please, I'm trying to tell you that I don't want you to leave."

Her mouth opened, but she didn't say anything for a long time. "You don't?"

He shook his head. "How could I, after you've devoted the past week to taking care of me? What kind of man would toss you and the kids out after all you've done?''

He raised a hand before she could speak. "Don't answer that. I know I haven't been the greatest patient. You've had to put up with a lot since my fall. If you're worried about me touching you again, you have my promise that won't happen. There is no reason why I can't continue to stay in the cottage and you and kids live here. Please, I'd like you to stay.''

Maura let out a sigh of relief. She'd been afraid to even hope for a reprieve. Of course there was still the problem of money, even more how this man affected her. She had to push aside these feelings and think about her children. "But I can't afford to pay rent and I can't take your charity, either.''

His voice was husky. "And I'm not giving it, Maura. I should be the one to pay you for nursing me. You didn't even go to work the first three days of this week. I owe you, Maura. Please stay… At least until you can afford to move out.''

"Okay, I will,'' Maura agreed, all the while knowing that when the time came, it was going to be even harder to leave. She'd come to care more for Wyatt far more than she should and she had no one to blame but herself.

Later that afternoon, Wyatt made his first trip downstairs since the day of the accident. And by God, he was going to make it on his own. Slowly, and with Kelly's encouragement he maneuvered the steps.

"You can do it, Wyatt,'' the three-year-old cheered as he paused on the landing to catch his breath. His strength was zapped. But after he got the okay from the doctor later today, he had to get back to work.

Kelly opened the door and the fresh country air smelled wonderful. He'd been inside too long.

"Hold my hand, Wyatt," Kelly said. "I'll help you go see your surprise." The girl's eyes widened and her tiny fingers covered her mouth as if she said something wrong.

"It's okay, Kelly," her mother assured her. "Why don't you help Wyatt outside?"

Wyatt was confused, but not for long. He stepped out on the porch to find that the floor had been sanded and varnished. He glanced toward the new railing and posts. They'd been painted a glossy white. The lawn was cleaned of any of the old porch wood and mowed, showing sprigs of green along with rows of colorful flowers lining the edge of the porch.

"Look this way, Wyatt," Kelly called.

When he turned around and looked up at the two-story house, he found that the entire structure gleamed with fresh white paint and the shutters were dark green, just as he'd planned to do.

"How do you like it, Wyatt?" Jeff asked. "We all helped, even Kelly."

Somehow Wyatt found his voice. "It looks great." He glanced at Maura unable to mask his shock. "You couldn't have done this all by yourself."

She shook her head. "No, someone had to keep you in bed," she said, then called over her shoulder, "c'mon out, guys."

Just then Chance, Cade, Travis and Jared appeared from beside the house, along with their wives and numerous kids carrying a roughly painted sign that read, Welcome To West Texas.

Wyatt swallowed back the sudden tightness in his

throat. He couldn't believe it. They had done all this? "Man, I don't know what to say."

"You don't have to say a thing, just offer us a drink." Cade walked up the steps. "And you also have to feed us."

Abby was right behind her husband. "Don't worry, Wyatt, we brought the food. You think you feel good enough to supervise the guys at the barbecue?"

"Sure." He was still unable to believe what the Randells had done. "Why would they do this?" he said to Maura, not realizing he'd spoken out loud.

Cade placed a gentle hand on Wyatt's shoulder. "Because we think if things were reversed, you'd come and help…a neighbor." He leaned closer. "In fact, you already did when you let Maura stay in the house. In my book that makes you an okay guy." Cade's mouth twitched. "Now, do you know how to barbecue prime Texas beef, or do I need to show you how a native does things?"

Wyatt's back was suddenly feeling much better. "Why don't you go and start up the grill, but I'll come to supervise? I just need to talk to Maura a second."

With Cade and Abby leading, the Randells headed through the house to the kitchen. Maura was about to follow with Jeff and Kelly when Wyatt called to her. She hung back, but sent the kids on.

She looked up at him expectantly. "Do you really like the house? I wasn't sure if I should let Cade and his brothers do it, but you had already bought the paint and…"

"It's great," he said. "Better than I could have hoped. It would have taken me weeks to finish. But thanks to you…" Wyatt couldn't seem to stop himself as he moved closer to her. This woman had been there for him, cared for him when he hadn't been such a nice guy.

"I'm glad you like it," she said. "Now you can concentrate on the barn and corral and bringing your stock here." She was acting shy with him again.

"Maura, look at me. Please," he found himself pleading.

She slowly raised those big bedroom eyes to him and he was lost. He tried to take a breath, but found he had trouble pulling air into his lungs. She made him forget everything he needed to think about. He had always been the practical one, now this woman drove every rational thought from his head. And yet, he didn't seem to mind one bit.

"Thank you, not just for this, but for everything." His voice lowered as did his head. "I couldn't have made it through this week if you hadn't been here to take care of me." Even when he'd been in the fog of drugs, he'd known she was at his side that first night. He recalled her touch as she helped him stand, the feel of her body against his as she helped him to the bathroom.

"I'm just happy I can pay back some of your kindness," she said.

There was laughter and the sound of loud voices in the house, but it didn't distract him. "I'm glad you're staying, Maura," he told her. "I would miss you and the kids."

She glanced away. "We'd miss you, too," she said, her voice barely a whisper.

He leaned closer, catching her familiar scent. "That's good to know." Their eyes met and he ached to close the distance and kiss her, but the promise he'd made to her lingered in the back of his mind. He couldn't break that trust. The last thing he wanted to do was scare her off. He cared about her too much to ever want to see her hurt again.

He wanted to show her how a real man could act. Someday. He backed away. Right now, he could wait until she was ready.

Chapter Seven

A flash of lightning zigzagged across the dark sky, followed by a loud clap of thunder. The rumbling sound seemed to vibrate the walls, though that wasn't what had kept Wyatt awake. The past week, ever since he'd moved back into the cottage, he hadn't been able to sleep worth a damn.

He finally got up from bed and slipped on his jeans, then walked to the small living room. At the window he watched as sheets of rain poured off the rickety porch. No doubt this area needed a gully washer, but could the cottage handle the storm? He knew the main house was stable, but what about the barn and the outer buildings? He made a mental note to check things out in the morning.

His concern was still on tonight...the storm. He looked toward the house and saw a light in Maura's bedroom. Was she frightened? Were the kids? He shook his head, telling himself they weren't his to worry about. Maura had made it clear several times that she could handle things on her own. She didn't need him...or any man.

How was he supposed to turn his feelings off? They'd been more or less been cohabiting for the past six weeks. They shared breakfast and supper together daily. He knew the name of Kelly's favorite doll, Suzy, and that Jeff had a talent for drawing pictures. For a six-year-old, he was pretty good, a talent he came by naturally.

He knew Maura had tried to shield more of herself from him. There was no doubt, she was an artistic person. Her flower arrangements had showed that, along with all the other special touches she'd made around the old house. He glanced over his shoulder, even in the cottage he could feel Maura's presence. She had turned the small, dingy rooms into an inviting place. She had found an old quilt in the attic. After washing it, she spread the colorful patchwork on his bed, and arranged fresh flowers on the scarred nightstand every time she came down to clean.

Everywhere he turned there was something to remind him of Maura. He should know from past experience with Amanda that he shouldn't get involved only to have her and the kids walk out of his life. But how could he keep Maura out of his head when she was in every nook and cranny of his life...of his heart?

There was another flash of lightning, along with a gust of wind, causing the cottage to shudder under its power. Wyatt drew a breath as he listened to the rain pelting down on his fragile roof. As a rule he liked storms. This one he wished was gone. But according to the weatherman, the storm front was going to last a while. Any more of these strong winds... He looked out just in time to see a part of the porch roof lift.

"Damn. I don't need this." He ran into the bedroom,

grabbed his shirt and pulled it on. When he heard a crash he hurried faster. He'd barely got his feet into his boots when he heard the sound of wood splitting. Hurrying back to the living room, he found water streaming in through a large hole in the roof that had been torn away. He grabbed a few things, and took off toward the house.

And Maura.

Maura sat on the bed trying to go over her monthly expenses. No matter what she did, she couldn't scrape together more than four hundred dollars a month for rent. She couldn't get even a one bedroom apartment that cheap, and she would still need first and last and a security deposit just to move in.

And what about utilities? She didn't have any money for them. This house already had the electricity and the water on. She paid for the phone herself, knowing she needed to be able to call for help. Just in case.

She could probably get state aid for Jeff and Kelly. Maybe she should call her mother. She shook her head. No, Grace Howell had turned her down before, not even wanting to see her own grandchildren.

A flash of lightning lit up the sky, making her more uncomfortable. She had few choices. No matter how many times she went over her finances, the bottom line never changed. The only other thing she could come up with was to ask Wyatt if she could rent the cottage. It was small but there were two bedrooms. Maybe he would let her continue to cook his meals and do his laundry for a cut in the rent. She didn't want to impose on the man any longer, but she didn't have any other options.

With another lightning flash, the lights flickered, then went out all together. Maura froze momentarily. She hated the dark, a reminder of how she'd tried to hide from Darren, but he'd always found her. She pushed the memory from her head and quickly got out of bed and lit the candle on the dresser. Once the soft glow appeared, she went to check on the kids. Luckily they were still asleep. She went downstairs to make sure things were secure. That was when she heard the pounding on the back door. She hurried through the kitchen and found Wyatt on the porch.

"Wyatt! What happened?" She stepped back to let him enter the dark kitchen.

He dropped the bundled quilt on the table, pulled off his hat and wiped the rain from his face. "The damn roof blew off the cottage."

"Oh, no," she cried, examining him more closely. "Were you hurt?"

"No, but the place is in shambles," he said. "Looks like I'm going to have to move back in here."

Maura swallowed her dismay. "Of course you can stay the night. Then tomorrow you can fix the roof."

"It's going to take longer than a day or two. I don't have the time to put in on repairing the structure. Don't worry, I figure I can stay in the small room off the kitchen." He pointed through the doorway.

"But it's a mess in there," she said. "Boxes and junk are piled everywhere." She had put a lot of it there herself.

"Then I guess I'll just have to clean it out," he said. "I'll buy a new bed and it'll be fine."

Although the room was dark, Wyatt could see Maura's discomfort. "Is there something wrong?"

"It's just that with all of us living here…it's not right. I think the kids and I should leave."

"And go where?" he asked.

"That's not your worry. We shouldn't have stayed here this long anyway."

She started to walk away and Wyatt stopped her. "Maura what's the real reason? Surely you're not afraid that I'll try something..."

She glanced away. "No, No, but people will talk..."

"Then let them. Besides, I stayed here when I hurt my back. In *your* bed."

"But that was different. You were injured."

He released a long breath. "Other than sleeping in the barn, I don't have a choice, Maura."

She still didn't look convinced. "How long before the roof can be repaired?"

"It's not going to be a simple job. The structure has damage. But the repairs are going to have to wait. My stock will be arriving in a few days."

This time she sighed. Where were she and the kids going to live now? "But...you don't understand."

"I guess I don't, Maura," he said. He was too tired to think about it tonight and a little hurt that she was so resistant to letting him stay. "I'll sleep on the sofa, unless you object to that, too." Not waiting for her answer, he marched into the dark living room and spread the quilt on the sofa.

She followed him. "I'm sorry, Wyatt. It's not fair to keep you out of your own home. It's just that I don't want the kids to get any ideas."

He turned around to find Maura standing there in her long cotton gown, the candle casting a soft glow over her face. She looked much the same as she had the night he first arrived, the same night he'd first been aroused by her.

"What kind of ideas?"

"I don't want them to think that you'll always be a

part of their lives," she confessed. "I also don't want them to think that you're a live-in boyfriend. I was married to their father, and he was the only man in our lives...until you."

Wyatt stepped closer. "You don't want people to think you're giving me special favors...in lieu of rent."

Even in the dim candlelight, he could see her blush.

He wanted so badly to pull her into his arms. "Maura, please believe me, I would never ask you... I care about you and the kids too much. But with this situation, I can't see there's any other answer. If you're worried about what people will think, tell 'em...that we're... engaged."

She gasped. "Oh, Wyatt. No!"

For some reason her reaction hurt. "Why? Jack Randell's bastard son isn't good enough?"

She looked as if he'd slapped her. "How could you think that? It's just that the kids would begin to get used to you being around all the time. And since we're leaving..."

He moved closer. "Why do you have to go, Maura? Why can't you stay here?"

"Because, this is your house, and you need to move in. The kids and I will just crowd you."

He raised an eyebrow. "Have I complained?"

"No, but it still isn't right."

His gaze met hers. "What if I wanted you to stay?"

Her breath caught. "But you can't want me..."

The hell he couldn't. He released a frustrated breath. "Ah, Maura, don't you know how special you are? How beautiful? Any man would be thrilled to have you in his life." He took the candle from her hand and set it on the coffee table, then reached out and cupped her cheek. He felt her tremble. "I don't know what your ex did to you, but not every man is cruel." She started to pull away, but he wouldn't let her. He bent his head, then paused before his mouth touched hers. She sucked in her breath. "Maura, let me show you how a man should treat a woman."

"Wyatt…" She breathed his name as her eyes closed.

Slowly, he drew her into his arms. "I would never hurt you, Maura. Never…"

The first kiss was gentle, then he pulled back, then dipped his head again and nibbled gently on her lower lip. "You taste good," he whispered, trying to slow his own fervor. It was difficult. "Ever since that first time I kissed you, I wanted to again and again."

Her gaze met his. He could see desire in those incredible whiskey-colored eyes of hers, but she wasn't ready to believe him. He didn't blame her. Trust came hard for him, too. He needed to take things slow, for the both of them. But right now, he wasn't exactly thinking rationally. Not when Maura was tempting him.

"Put your hands on me, Maura. Touch me."

His shirt hung open and he was still wet from the rain. When her warm fingers raked across his flesh he nearly came apart. He groaned and placed his hands over hers. "Woman, you do unbelievable things to me."

"Really?" She sounded surprised.

"Really," he repeated, right before he captured her mouth in another kiss. When she didn't resist, he ran his tongue over the seam of her lips. With a soft whimper, she opened for him and allowed him inside to taste her again. By the time he finally broke off the kiss, they were both breathing hard.

He smiled, despite his agony. "That was nice."

"Nice," she repeated, then surprised him when she raised up on her toes and pressed her mouth to his. He couldn't resist the invitation to intensify the kiss. This time she kissed him back, mimicking everything he did to her. When he reached out to touch her breasts, she gasped.

A lightning flash illuminated the room momentarily. "I want you, Maura."

"Wyatt..." She whispered his name when suddenly the sound of a child's cry filled the room.

She jerked back. "Kelly." Grabbing the candle, Maura hurried upstairs and Wyatt followed her.

They reached the bedroom to find the tiny girl sitting up in bed sobbing.

"I'm scared, Mommy," Kelly cried. "I'm scared a bad man is coming to get me."

"Shh, baby," her mother soothed her, wrapping her arms around her child. "You're okay now."

"I'm here, too, princess," Wyatt said as he moved to the bed. "And I'm not going to let anything bad happen to you."

Wyatt looked down at Maura holding her child. Something tightened around his heart and he knew that he'd kill anyone who would ever try to hurt them.

Wyatt woke up early the next morning to bright sunlight and found last night's storm had left a lot of damage in its wake. He went out to examine the destruction. The newly painted house had held up very well, but he'd lost a few trees and the cottage had sustained a lot of damage. The repairs were going to take a lot more time and money than he wanted to spend at the moment.

He needed to focus his energy on other things. He had two days to get the barn and corrals ready for the horses, Rock-a-Billy and Stormy Weather. His friend, Bud Wilks, was also bringing along a few other horses that he told Wyatt were promising. Since Bud was going to be his manager, Wyatt trusted his judgement on the stock. He couldn't help but be excited about how things were moving forward, but at the moment bucking horses were the last thing on his mind.

Maura was the first.

What would have happened last night if Kelly hadn't woken up? Would Maura have let him make love to her? Deep down, he knew she wasn't ready. Maybe she'd never be ready to let him into her life. He knew that she'd been abused by her husband. Maybe she would never let another man get close again. She had kissed him back. Did he want to go to the next step? He had to be damn sure that he wanted it all. Maura Wells wasn't the kind of woman a man took to bed and just walked away from.

Wyatt wasn't sure about love. He'd been hurt before and decided that a permanent relationship might not be in the cards for him. All he knew was that he wanted Maura here, in his life.

Kelly pushed open the screen door and stepped out to the porch. The little pixie was so cute dressed in a little red skirt and white shirt. Maura wasn't the only female in the house who had stolen his heart.

"Hi, Wyatt." She smiled shyly. "Mom says that breakfast is ready."

"It is?" he said walking toward her. "What are we having this morning?"

"Mommy's fixin' me pancakes 'cause I got scared last night."

He sat down on the edge of the porch. "I know. Did you have a bad dream?"

She nodded. Tears filled her beautiful eyes. "Don't let the bad man get me, Wyatt, please."

He took her in his arms. "Shh, princess. I promise, I'll never let anyone hurt you."

Kelly's tiny arms circled his neck. "Good. You know what?"

"What?"

"I wish we can stay here forever and ever. So I don't hafta be scared anymore."

Wyatt choked back an angry comment. What kind of father had Maura's ex been? "I'm not sure your mother will go for that idea."

"You could marry Mommy."

Whoa. How was he going to answer that one? Think quick. "How can I marry your mother when I'm plannin' to marry you?"

She giggled. "But I'm a little girl."

"Then I'll just wait until you grow up."

Maura called for her daughter and Kelly got up and headed inside. Wyatt sat for a while. Marriage. Not just to take a wife, but if he wanted Maura, he had a ready-made family.

He thought about his own mother, raising him and Dylan without any help from the man who'd fathered them. Who didn't want them. Growing up, Wyatt had always felt there was part of him missing, never knowing exactly who he was. Now that he learned about Randell, he didn't feel any better. His chest tightened. Maybe that's the reason he seemed to relate to Jeff and Kelly.

All kids need a father who cares.

Realizing the direction of his thoughts, he shook away the crazy notion. What the hell did he know about being someone's daddy?

Wyatt stood and went into the kitchen and found Maura at the stove. She was dressed for work in a dark skirt and a fitted white cotton top. Her blond hair was pulled away from her face and held with clips. She looked tired. She probably hadn't gotten any more sleep than he had.

She finally glanced at him and his pulse rate sped up. He smiled. "Good morning."

"Good morning," she said. "Was there any more damage from the storm?"

He shook his head and sat down in his usual seat at the table. "Just the cottage and a few trees."

Maura handed him a mug of coffee. "Pancakes all right?"

"They're my favorite." He winked at Kelly who was already eating. Jeff walked into the room and sat down.

"How did you sleep, Jeff?" Wyatt asked. "Did the storm wake you?"

"No, I wasn't scared." he insisted a little too quickly.

"I sure was," Wyatt admitted. "When the roof blew off the cottage and I came running to the house."

"Wyatt's gonna live with us," Kelly said. She pointed toward the utility room. "He's sleeping in there."

Jeff jerked his attention back to Wyatt. "Are you staying here for good? Do we have to leave?"

Wyatt shook his head seeing the boy's panic. "No, you don't have to leave. I just need a place to sleep until the cottage gets repaired. Maybe we can work on it together. What do ya say, Jeff?"

He shrugged. "Maybe." He turned to his mother. "You sure we're not leaving?"

She peered at Wyatt for a moment. "You know we can't stay here permanently." She sighed. "I'm going to look for apartments after work."

"But Mom, I want to live here," Kelly said. "My room is pretty and Wyatt says we can stay."

"Kelly, finish your breakfast."

"I don't want any more," she said and lowered her head.

"Then go upstairs and brush your teeth. Jeff, you, too."

The boy started to speak, then changed his mind. "C'mon, Kelly. I'll help you," he said and took his sister's hand and they left the kitchen.

When had Maura made the decision to leave? Wyatt wondered. "Why are you doing this to the kids?" Wyatt asked. To me? "I told you that you can stay here as long as you need."

"And I told you that I can't keep taking your charity."

"It's not charity, dammit! You work harder than two people around here. Can't we share this large house?"

"Can't you see that it's only going to be harder when I have to go? And I was planning to leave. I'd decided to ask you about renting the cottage, but as of now it looks like I can't do that." She got up from the table and turned away from him.

Wyatt got up, too. "Maura, please. I care about you and the kids. Is it because I kissed you last night?"

"That was a mistake," she said, then moved across the room. "I don't want you to think that just because I'm handy I'll go to bed with you."

"And you honestly believe that I would take advantage of you like that? In the past few weeks, have I tried to take advantage of our situation? I thought that kiss was mutual. I thought you wanted it as much as I did. I guess I read your signals wrong." He stood behind her, but kept his hands to himself.

"Believe me, Maura. I would never intentionally do anything to hurt you or the kids." He stared at her stiff back, knowing he wasn't getting through to her. "Ah, hell, think what you want.'' He started for the back door, then stopped. ''Just don't mistake me for your ex-husband.''

Two days later, Maura was going stir crazy. She hadn't seen Wyatt since the scene in the kitchen. She knew she might have been a little unfair to him. He was right; he wasn't anything remotely like Darren. But that was just it. What if Darren *did* find her? Knowing her ex-husband, he wouldn't stop until he got what he wanted: revenge. How could she let someone as kind and wonderful as Wyatt into the mess she'd made of her life?

But she couldn't stay away from him any longer. With her children spending the day with Abby and her kids, she went in search of him. Not finding him at the cottage, she wandered down to the barn. Inside, she saw that each stall had been cleaned out and lined with fresh straw.

She walked down the center aisle, following the sound of a country and western song coming from the tack room. The door was open and she found the place to be neat and clean. A scarred desk was along one wall on top was a phone and several folders were stacked and orderly. Another wall was a cot where Wyatt sat busy polishing one of the bridles that hung on the wall.

Dressed in faded jeans and a chambray shirt, he looked wonderful. Her stomach began to flutter. Oh, how she'd missed him.

He looked up, no doubt surprised to see her. ''Maura, is something wrong?'' He got up from the bunk.

She shook her head, biting at her lip. ''Oh, Wyatt, this is where you've been sleeping. I feel so awful.''

Wyatt went to her, still having trouble believing that

she came to him. "It's all right, Maura. It hasn't been so bad. I've cleaned up the place pretty good," he said, recalling the late hours he spent on the room when he couldn't sleep.

"I'm sorry," she said, her eyes sad. "Please, come back to the house. You belong there."

He wanted that more than anything. "No, because if I do, you'll leave. And I don't want you to leave."

"I don't want to leave…either" A lone tear found its way down her cheek. "I was scarred, Wyatt." She swiped at the moisture on her face. "There are things…you don't know about my life."

"No, I don't," he confirmed, "but I figure when you're ready you'll tell me."

"I don't know if I'll ever be able to."

"That's okay, too." He brushed a wayward curl from her face, aching to take her in his arms. "I'm not going anywhere." He just realized that he was making a commitment to her.

"Will you move back to the house?"

"Why should I?"

"Because I don't care what people say. I want you to."

Wyatt grinned. "That's all I wanted to hear." He sobered. "I don't want you to feel uncomfortable with me around."

Being uncomfortable wasn't what Maura was worried about. She didn't need to get involved with this man, for his sake more than hers. But she couldn't seem to stop the feelings he created in her. "I won't be uncomfortable," she fibbed. "But I think we shouldn't… I mean we can't let what happened the other night happen again."

He cocked an eyebrow. "Are you talking about the kiss?"

She nodded.

"The kiss that we both enjoyed, and I might add seemed to take a lot of pleasure in."

"Wyatt, please! I have children who could be watching."

"Dammit, woman. I happen to like kissing you."

She sucked in a breath as a shiver ran through her. She did, too. No, she couldn't let anything more happen.

Wyatt stepped closer. "Okay, but how about one last kiss?" he asked in a low husky voice as he lowered his head. He paused just inches from her.

The sound of a throat being cleared caused them both to turn to the door and found Hank Barrett standing in the doorway.

"Hank," Maura said as heat flooded her face. "I didn't know you were coming by."

"I apologize for disturbing you." Hank's grin widened.

Wyatt refused to let Maura leave his side. "What can I do for you, Hank?"

"Well, first of all, there seems to be a caravan of trucks coming up your driveway."

"So they finally made it," Wyatt said, then took off. Once outside the barn he spotted Bud's green truck and horse trailer. Behind him was his friend, Dusty Adams, with another truck and trailer.

Wyatt went to greet Bud. "Hey, welcome to Texas. Have any trouble getting here?"

"Thanks. We hit some bad weather that slowed us down a little. I think we should get these fellas unloaded."

"Sure. Let's put them in the corral so they can get

some exercise.'' Wyatt followed Bud to the trailer and they dropped the gate. He walked up the ramp and un-hooked the lead rope to the bay horse and backed him out. Bud followed with the buckskin. Wyatt stopped when he noticed Hank's interest in the spirited animals.

''Hank, meet Stormy Weather, and this guy is Rock-a-Billy. These two are some of the best bucking broncs around.'' He patted the animal on his neck. ''I especially have high hopes for this guy. Could be a contender for horse of the year.''

Hank ran his hand over the hind quarters as the horse danced sideways. ''How do you feel about trying him out locally?''

''Where would that be?''

''At the Annual Circle B Rodeo.''

Chapter Eight

Two days later, Wyatt stood at the pasture fence and watched his horses graze. They seemed to be getting used to their new home, but they weren't going to be lazing around the ranch for long. Eventually, they'd be making money for him. He'd already signed contracts for two local rodeos for the early spring. Next month, they were headed to southern Arizona, then on to California for bigger events. He was still small time, but hopefully that would change when word of Stormy Weather and Rock-a-Billy got around.

There was no doubt in Wyatt's mind that in a few months, his two broncs would make a name for him. He'd been on the rodeo circuit all his life and he'd learned a few things about good stock. The one and only good thing about Earl Keys, the gruff old man had taught him the business. And in his gut, Wyatt knew these horses had what it took.

A cloud of dust kicked up in the distance and alerted Wyatt that someone was headed for the ranch. Hank Barrett's truck pulled up next to the barn and he climbed out. With his posture erect, the large man tugged on his Stetson, then started his long sure strides toward Wyatt. Hank didn't look anywhere near his age.

"Good morning," the older rancher said.

"Good morning." Wyatt returned. "You're out early."

"I hope you don't mind. I forget that not everyone is up with the sun."

"I was up. I have stock to feed now."

Hank squinted against the bright sun as he looked around. "This place is shapin' up real good. If I didn't know better, I'd swear your granddad, John Randell, was still runnin' things. All you need is a few hundred head of good Texas steers."

Wyatt laughed. "I'm not a rancher, Hank."

"Well, your grandpa John was a helluva one. He was also a good friend of mine." Hank sobered. "It's a shame his son, Jack, didn't inherit a few of his qualities."

"Does anyone know where he is?"

The lines around Hank's hazel eyes deepened as he squinted into the sun. "Jack Randell isn't exactly welcome in these parts. There's a few people who still believe that a cattle rustler should be strung up. That might not be the news you want to hear, but you had to know that your daddy's character was…questionable. He was married when he was with your mother."

"Yeah, but kids always have silly notions about turning their old man into a hero." Wyatt couldn't believe he was spilling his guts.

"None of us are perfect, son. I did the best I could with the boys. If you're looking for a hero, like I said, your granddaddy was quite a man."

Wyatt was amazed how easily Hank had accepted him.

Hank gave him a questioning look. "Something wrong?"

Wyatt shook his head. "It's just that since I've arrived here, you've treated me so fairly. You don't seem to think I have some ulterior motive."

The older rancher turned to the pasture, rested his arms across the top fence railing and looked out at the horses. "I'm not as trusting as you might think. When Jared showed up here, I did some checking. Jared showed me the private investigator's report on you and Dylan. I was curious about you buying this place, but you were right. The price was too good to pass up." He tossed a glance toward Wyatt. "My concern has always been the same. I don't want Chance, Cade and Travis hurt. They've gone through hell because of Jack."

Wyatt found he truly envied his half brothers to have this man's love. "They consider you their father."

Emotion showed in Hank's eyes. "And I love them as if they were my own. I've always said you don't have to be blood to be family. About a year ago I discovered that I had fathered a child years ago, a daughter. After her mother died, Josie came to the ranch to find me." He smiled. "She's married to Travis."

"It must be nice to have a large family."

"There's nothing stopping you from having the same," Hank said. He nodded toward the house. "I know there's one pretty filly that's already caught your eye."

Wyatt was confused about how he felt about Maura. "A ready-made family might be a little more than I can take on."

Hank shrugged. "I'd call it a bonus. That's how

Chance got Katie Rose and Travis got Elissa Mae. Kids don't ask for blood tests from their parents, just love and being there for them.''

"How does a man know if he can handle the job?''

"How hard is it to give to a boy who already idolizes you and a little girl who's crazy about you?''

Wyatt couldn't think of anything to say.

"And Maura has had enough pain to last a lifetime. She needs a gentle touch and a man who is willing to love her. But I guess if you're not up to the task, there'll be someone who'll be willing to give her what she needs.''

Wyatt stiffened, hating the possibility. He didn't want another man kissing her, making love to her.

Just then Maura walked out the back door with Kelly. She was headed to work. That meant that she'd be gone all day. She waved and helped Kelly into the car, then drove off.

"This place must get pretty lonely with no one around all day. Just think about the nights once Maura and the kids leave.''

"I know what you're trying to do, Hank,'' Wyatt said. And dammit, it was working.

"Just stating some facts,'' Hank assured him. "I came over to see if you'll let me contract your stock for the Circle B Rodeo.''

"You haven't gotten your rough-stock supplier yet?''

"We've had some problems, so I told them to forget it.'' He sighed. "I know it's a small time rodeo, Wyatt, but I thought maybe you'd want to show off your new broncs.''

"Sounds good. And I'll do it with one condition—that you stop playing matchmaker.''

"Oh, I don't have to play anything." The man grinned. "You're already a goner. You just haven't admitted it yet."

"Mom, you're not listening to me," Jeff insisted.

"What, honey?" Maura broke out of her reverie. "Did you say something?

"You need to sign my printing homework."

She took the pencil from Jeff and wrote her name on the space available. "I'm sorry, I must be tired."

"That's okay. I know you work hard."

Maura was happy that her son thought so. But the real reason she had been so absentminded was Wyatt. Her gaze had been glued to the back door, wondering when he was going to come in for the night. It seemed he'd been spending more and more time away from the house. She understood he had animals to care for, but that didn't change the fact that she missed him, especially after Jeff and Kelly went to bed.

And she was alone.

Not that she didn't have enough work to keep her busy with cooking and the kids. She needed to concentrate on her general business assignments and help Jeff with his schoolwork, not think about a rodeo cowboy.

Suddenly the screen door opened, Wyatt walked in and placed his hat on a nearby hook. Maura's breath caught as her hungry gaze moved over him. He was in dirty, worn jeans and a shirt that had been torn and there was a day's growth of whiskers covering his square jaw. He looked wonderful.

"Sorry, I didn't mean to disturb you," he said. "I'll just wash up and get out of your hair." He went to the sink and began washing his hands.

Jeff got up from the chair. "I finished my words. See?"

Wyatt smiled. "Hey, that's pretty good." He grabbed the towel off the rack and wiped his hands.

"Now, will you let me see the bulls?" the boy asked.

Wyatt hung up the towel. "How about tomorrow after you get home?"

Jeff frowned. "But it's dark then."

"Then you'll have to wait until Saturday," Maura said.

Wyatt saw the boy's disappointment, but there wasn't much he could do. "Sorry, Jeff, I guess that's how it has to be. But I'll have another surprise for you and your sister by then."

The boy's eyes lit up, reminding Wyatt of Maura. "What?"

"If I tell you, it won't be a surprise, will it?"

"But Saturday is two days away."

"Maybe you better get to bed so it'll come faster," his mother said and waved him toward the door. "I'll be up shortly."

Jeff smiled at Wyatt. "Night." He hurried off.

Wyatt turned to Maura, but she quickly glanced away and busied herself putting Jeff's homework in his backpack.

"Maura, are you worried about having the bulls here?"

"I'm not crazy about them, but it's your business."

"I've made sure they're in the best reinforced pens and the pasture is secured, too. They aren't going to get out. Besides, if they aren't hassled they're pretty mild."

She gave him an incredulous look. "Even I'm not that naive."

"Maura, it's safe. I've taken every precaution. Believe me, for what I paid for them, I don't want those bulls out any more than you do."

Wyatt had built the bulls' pen way behind the barn to keep them out of view of the house. With Bud here to care for the stock until he left for the circuit at the beginning of the year, Wyatt had help getting more things done around the ranch. First on the list was to repair the cottage, then maybe build a bunkhouse so he could hire on help. And Wyatt had been thinking a lot about Hank's idea of raising cattle.

Maura finally nodded. "I guess you're right," she admitted, then glanced away.

"Is there something else bothering you?" She hadn't really looked at him since the day in the barn when he'd nearly kissed her. That was seven long days ago.

"I went to the paint store today and picked out some color chips for the living room and dining room walls. They're in your room," she said.

"Good, I'll have a look, but I'm going to leave the choosing up to you. So what else is bothering you?"

"I know you've been busy, but I was wondering if I've done something to make you angry."

Not angry, but frustrated as hell. He leaned against the old sink to keep from pulling her into his arms and showing her how badly he wanted her.

"No, you didn't do anything wrong," he said. "I've just been busy with the stock." The distraction still hadn't kept him from thinking about her. But he had to be fair to Maura. She needed a man who was ready to give her a commitment. He wasn't sure he was that man. He'd been down that road and ended up getting burned. But dammit, that didn't stop him from wanting her.

"Maura, I care about you…"

She raised those brown eyes to his and he had to swallow the sudden dryness in his throat. "But I don't think either of us are ready for something long-term."

He watched as she bit down on her lower lip, and he remembered how sweet she tasted. He held on to his resolve and kept his distance.

"Of course you're right," she agreed. "And I have children to think about." She went to the table and picked up the clutter. "I need to go check on Jeff and Kelly." Books hugged against her chest like a shield, she faced him "So... I guess I'll see you in the morning. Good night."

An empty feeling came over Wyatt as he watched Maura walk out of the room. No matter how much he cared for her, he had to let her go. He wasn't ready to risk his heart again, but he knew deep down that it was already too late. Maura Wells had already stolen it.

Saturday morning an excited Jeff and Kelly were out of bed at dawn. Maura had overslept and when she reached the kitchen, Wyatt had already started breakfast for Bud and the kids.

She hugged her robe tighter. "I'm sorry. I guess I forgot to set my alarm." She walked to the stove and tried to take over for Wyatt. He nudged her away.

"Why don't you let me handle it this morning?"

"Yeah, Mom," Kelly chimed in. "We're going to make breakfast. Scrambled eggs and bacon."

"It's a cowboy's breakfast," Jeff added.

Wyatt winked at her. "Here, have some coffee." He handed her a mug. "Why don't you go and take some time for yourself? We have things under control here."

She glanced down at robe. "Do I look that bad?"

He turned her around, back to where she'd come from. "No, you look too good," he whispered against her ear, causing little shivers along her skin. "Now go and change, and I'll have a surprise for you when you get back.''

After breakfast and with the kitchen cleaned in record time, Wyatt and Bud asked for ten minutes before she brought the kids down to the barn. Both Jeff and Kelly were going crazy by the time Maura told them it was time to go.

Jeff cheered as he banged open the screen door and ran out to the porch, then stopped and came back to help his sister.

Maura could feel her own excitement as she hurried to keep up. At the barn door, Maura called out. "Wyatt, we're here," she said, recalling that she hadn't been inside since the day she'd asked Wyatt to move back into the house. That was ten days ago.

Wyatt came toward them. "You guys ready?"

"Yes!" Jeff called.

"Oh, yes, Wyatt," Kelly said as she jumped up and down.

"Okay, Bud bring out Sandy."

The slightly built cowboy with the easy smile walked out of the shadows leading a caramel-colored pony with a bleached-blond mane and tail. She was saddled and ready to take riders.

Neither Jeff and Kelly could contain their excitement.

Maura wasn't sure what to do as she looked at Wyatt.

"This is Sandy," he said, "She's from the Circle B. Hank said she hasn't been ridden much lately and he thinks she needed a couple of kids to spend time with."

"So she's used to kids?" Maura asked, nodding toward the small animal.

"She's as gentle as an old dog." He rubbed the pony's neck, then showed Kelly and Jeff how to pet her.

"See, Mom, Sandy likes me," Kelly said and demonstrated by rubbing the animal's face.

"Here, feed her some sugar," Wyatt gave each child one cube and demonstrated how to feed the pony.

"Mom, can we ride her?" Jeff asked.

Wyatt cocked an eyebrow as if asking for her okay. She knew in her heart that he'd never put her children in danger. It sometimes amazed her how much she trusted him.

"I think it will be all right, if Wyatt walks with you around the corral."

"That's what I planned," he promised.

"Ladies first." Wyatt lifted Kelly onto the saddle and put her feet into the stirrups, then started to lead the pony out of the barn. As he passed Maura, he leaned down and said, "Don't go wandering off, I have plans for you later."

Another tingle shot through Maura as she took her son's hand and walked to the corral fence. They climbed onto the top railing. She watched the kids' excitement as Wyatt took turns with them both. Maura's trust grew and she allowed Jeff to take the pony's reins and go on his own, as long as Wyatt was there beside the animal.

"Mommy, look," Kelly cried and she pointed to the barn.

Over her shoulder, Maura turned and saw Bud come out leading another horse. This time it was a big, black stallion.

"Wyatt, is that your horse Raven?" Jeff asked.

"That's him." Wyatt grinned proudly. "He got here yesterday while you were at school."

How did the kids know about Wyatt's horse? The realization made Maura feel a little left out.

Wyatt had Jeff climb down off the pony, then he am-

led over and swapped animals with Bud. Both children
at with her on the railing. "Wyatt, make him do his
ricks," Jeff called out.

They watched as Wyatt took the animal to the center
f the arena. "What do you say, Raven? You want to
lo some tricks for Maura, Jeff and Kelly?"

The horse began moving his head up and down, mak-
ng the kids laugh. Then Wyatt placed his booted foot
nto the stirrup and easily swung into the saddle. With
a cocky grin that would leave any woman weak-kneed,
Wyatt adjusted his hat, then tugged on the reins and the
horse spun around in a circle. When he moved the reins
o the other side and the horse reversed directions. Jeff
and Kelly clapped their hands. Raven had only begun.
He reared back, kicking dust up. Then the magnificent
animal rose on his hind legs, peddling his front legs in
the air. The kids went crazy and Maura was captivated
with the performance. But her interest was focused on
the cowboy seated on the powerful animal.

Wyatt enjoyed watching the kids having a good time.
He realized, too, how much he'd missed having Raven
around this past month. Finally he had found a perma-
ent home for both of them.

"Do some more tricks, Wyatt," Kelly cried.

Wyatt decided that Maura had been missing out on
all the fun. He walked the horse to the railing. "Oh, I
hink it's time that your mother had a chance to ride."
He reached over and wrapped his arm around Maura's
waist, plucking her from the railing and onto the horse.

She gasped. "Wyatt, no, I can't."

"Just relax," he said as he held her slender body in
ront of his. "Now, swing your leg over the saddle.
That's it," he coaxed. "Just sit down in front of me."

He gave her the saddle and he slipped onto the rump o
the horse.

"Wyatt, you're crazy!" she exclaimed.

He wrapped his arms around her rib cage, just unde
her breasts and his body stirred instantly. Yeah, he wa
crazy. He certainly wasn't listening to his commo
sense. But no matter how hard he tried to stay away, h
was drawn to her. Was that so bad? Was it so bad tha
he wanted her, he wanted to touch her…to hold her? H
looked at the Jeff and Kelly sitting on the fence and fel
a strange protectiveness toward them. Was this how i
felt to have a real family? If so, he liked it. A lot.

"Why don't we do a little showing off for Jeff an
Kelly?"

"I want to get down," she said tensely.

"Maura, you have to know that I would never le
anything happen to you," he whispered against her ear
inhaling the clean scent of her hair, feeling her softnes
against him.

Maura looked over her shoulder, her dark eyes sen
sual, yet trusting. "I know," she said and didn't pul
back. She was so close all he had to do was move mer
inches and he could kiss that tempting mouth of hers
Realizing what he was thinking, he straightened and pat
ted the horse's neck.

"Hey, Raven here is a sweet guy. Aren't you
buddy?"

The animal raised his head up and whinnied loudly
Everyone laughed, including Maura. Finally she relaxe
back against him.

Then she smiled, sending his pulse pounding loudl
in his ears. "Okay, cowboy, take me for a ride," sh
said.

"My pleasure, ma'am," he said, taking the reins an

moving closer to her, cuddling her against his chest. Oh, he was enjoying this.

"This is fun."

"It's more fun if you take the reins." He demonstrated how to hold the leather straps. "Now, you're in control."

"What do I do?"

"Raven responds to both touch and voice commands. If you move the reins right or left he'll go in that direction. Make a clicking sound with your tongue and he walks. Kick your heels into his side and he'll take off. Tug on the reins and he'll stop."

"So you just have to know what gear to put him in," Maura said, trying to hide a smile.

Wyatt was dumbfounded hearing Maura's joke. And he wondered how long it had been since she took time to enjoy herself. He poked her in the ribs and discovered she was ticklish and had a contagious laugh.

"You should do that more often."

"What's that?" She laughed again. "Ride a horse?"

"That, too, but I meant laugh." He tugged his hat lower and watched her go through the routine. She seemed pretty pleased with herself once she had circled the corral on her own.

"Pretty good for a greenhorn."

She sucked in a breath. "I'd say it's *very* good for my first time on a horse."

"Yeah, Mom, you're great," Jeff said.

"Hey, Maura," Bud called to her, holding the pony's reins. "Is it okay if I let the kids help me brush down Candy?"

"I guess it's okay," she said. "Jeff, watch your sister, and Kelly, stay with Jeff." Both children nodded and followed Bud and the small horse into the barn.

"You don't have to worry, Bud'll take care of them.

She released a sigh. "It's just that they've never bee around animals."

"You lived in the city all your life?"

"Yes, and the kids, too. They've never even had dog."

"I take it your husband didn't like animals." Wya felt Maura stiffen. "Hey, I'm not trying to pry, just mal ing conversation."

"No, Darren didn't like animals...or kids."

Raven shifted and Wyatt set him walking agai "Maybe it's better for all of you that he's out of you life."

"I wish that were true," she mumbled.

He stopped the horse in the shade beside the barn "Maura, I know that you haven't talked much abou your marriage, and I'm not going to ask anything abou the past. But I have to know, would you ever conside going back to him?"

Her eyes grew large and filled with tears. "Never! I' do anything to keep him away from the kids."

"Ssh..." Wyatt wrapped his arms around her an pulled her trembling body against his chest. "I won't l him hurt you, Maura. Never again," he promised.

"You don't know him, Wyatt, or what he's capabl of doing."

"I know as long as I'm around, he's never going t hurt you or the kids." God, he ached to get his hand on this guy.

Maura's gaze locked with his. "You can't make promise like that, Wyatt. Darren *will* come after me. H swore he would, so I can't stay in one place too lon It would be better if I moved on."

Wyatt felt a panic like never before experienced, not even when Amanda left him. "You can't run away."

"It is if it's the only way I can survive. I have my children to think about."

"Then don't leave. I can protect you here. Bud's going to help me repair the cottage. It should only take a few weeks and then you and the kids can move in."

He watched her eyes light up. "I thought you said you weren't going to do the work just yet."

"If it keeps you safe and here, I'll do about anything. So I'll rent it to you. Just stay, Maura."

"But— I—"

"Just listen a minute. I'm not asking you to jump into anything. Just spend some time with you."

She hesitated for another second. "I'd like that," she finally said.

He released a breath. "Okay, how about the Circle B Rodeo?"

"What about it?"

"How about if I ask you to go…as my date?"

Chapter Nine

Hank stood next to the corral and watched as the men finished setting up the stock pens for the day's events. He'd been up since 4:00 a.m. making sure everything was ready, and Chance, Cade and Travis had worked until well after midnight last night.

Funny, the Circle B Rodeo had started out as a way to get the boys involved in something and over the last twenty years it had grown into a full-fledged rodeo. Although all the events were for amateurs, more and more of the local ranch hands entered each year and over three hundred people were expected to attend today. Just the thought of all those people to feed made Hank tired, but he loved putting on this rodeo. At sixty-six, he had considered retiring, handing the reins over to the boys to continue the tradition. He sighed. But he wasn't ready to let it go just yet.

Hearing his name called, Hank turned to see Ella hurrying toward him. She was dressed in her usual jeans and Western blouse. Her gray hair was cut short and combed away from her heart-shaped face. Nearly sixty, she was a handsome woman with expressive eyes. It had taken him awhile but he'd learned to read her moods, and stayed out of her way when she got out of sorts.

For the past twenty-five years she had run the house like a drill sergeant, but he'd never questioned her love for Chance, Cade and Travis. She'd raised those boys as if they were her own, and treated the grandkids the same. The woman had been around for so long he couldn't imagine the place without her.

"Hank, I need some of the men to help set up tables." She placed her hands on her hips. "Those high-school kids Chance hired never showed this morning. And I don't want any of the ladies to lift heavy things."

"I don't, either," he said. "They should be concentrating on the food."

She shook her head, fighting a smile, as she glanced at his waistline. He knew it drove her crazy that he never put on any weight. "Is that all you ever think about? Food?" she demanded.

"On a day like today, I get to sample heaven. Did Claire Watson bring her cheesy potatoes?"

Ella huffed. "Of course. That woman would do anything to catch herself a man."

Hank knew that was true, and he steered clear of widow Watson, but not of her potatoes. "What's wrong with trying to please a man?" he asked.

"A woman can please a man without having to cook for him."

He shrugged. "What else does a man my age have to think about, but food?"

"If I got to tell you, Hank Barrett, maybe you are too old." She winked at him, then turned and sauntered off.

A strange feeling came over him. "What the devil is

the woman takin' about?'' he mumbled to himself. He
pushed aside the thought and looked up to see Wyatt
Gentry's truck pull up beside the barn.

Wyatt climbed down from the truck cab then helped
Jeff out of the back seat. Before he let the boy go, he
made him promise not to hang around the rodeo pen
unless he was with an adult. Jeff agreed, then took off
to find his friends.

Wyatt had delivered the rough stock early this morning when none of the neighbors were around. This would
be his first return to the Circle B since his identity became public knowledge. There would probably be some
who'd question him about his relationship to the Randells.

He walked to the rear of the truck and dropped the
tailgate to help unload the boxes of food Maura had
spent all last night preparing for the barbecue. She and
Kelly came up beside him. Looking at him with those
big brown eyes, Maura smiled. ''It's going to be al-
right, Wyatt.''

''What's going to be all right?''

''You're worried about today,'' she said. ''Your bucking broncs will be great. And of course some people will
probably ask questions about Jack, but your brothers will
be there.''

He'd never thought himself easy to read, but he didn't
seem to be able to hide anything from Maura. ''How did
you know it was bothering me?''

She smiled in that warm way of hers and his body
temperature shot up. ''You've been frowning since you
got into the truck.''

''Maybe I was just squinting because of the sun.''

''Maybe,'' she agreed as Kelly tugged on her arm.

"Mommy, I want to go play with Katie."

"Okay, honey, but you have to stay in the play area. There are too many people and trucks around."

"I will, I promise." She drew an X over her heart, then took off toward the fenced area sectioned off for the younger kids, with adults taking turns supervising the kids.

"She'll be okay," Wyatt said.

"I know." She looked toward the house. "I guess I should take my potato salad and green bean casserole inside."

He stopped her when she went to reach for the box. "Maura, now it's your turn. Tell me what's bothering you?"

"Nothing's bothering me," she claimed, but they both knew she was lying.

His eyes held hers. "I think you're concerned about what people are going to say about us living together."

He'd liked staying in the house these past weeks, being with Maura and the kids. Although he hadn't touched her, he desperately wanted to. Even knowing he could be headed for heartbreak again, he still wanted a chance to see where it could lead.

"There's nothing we can do about that, Wyatt."

"Well, you could tell them that you and kids are going to rent the cottage." He didn't like the idea of them crowded into that tiny place, but he'd do just about anything to keep her close by.

She finally smiled briefly. "But people will see us together and just assume that we…"

He leaned closer. "I can't help it that when you look at me it turns me every way but loose."

She blushed. "Maybe I should stop looking at you."

"Or stop worrying about what people think."

"Look who's talking. Hold your head up, Wyatt Gentry, you have nothing to be ashamed of. You are a good man."

"Then trust me. You stay in the house where there's more room and I'll move out to the cottage."

"Oh, Wyatt, I can't let you do that."

"What if the circumstances were different?"

Her eyes widened. "What do you mean?"

Yeah, what did he mean? Before he could come up with something, Chance called to him.

Wyatt excused himself, walked a few feet away to speak with Chance. By the time he got back, Maura was already carrying one of the boxes into the house. He grabbed another and followed her.

Once inside the large Circle B kitchen he paused and watched dozens of women chatting while busily preparing the food. Being the new guy in the area, he didn't know any of them, but Maura was greeted warmly by the neighbors. Then Ella noticed his presence.

"Well, ladies, will you look at what has wandered in," the housekeeper declared. "He's a handsome devil just like his brothers, wouldn't you say? How are you doin', Wyatt?"

"Fine, thank you," he said as he deposited his box on the counter. He started off when Ella called to him again.

"I hear you're supplying the rough stock today."

"Yeah, I hope no one is disappointed."

Another woman waved her hand in the air. "Hey, today is all for fun. The men just want bragging rights for the next year. We only pray no one gets hurt."

Maura smiled as she walked by. "I told you so," she said and headed out the door.

He followed her outside and back to the truck to get more cartons.

She walked briskly to the truck. "Wyatt, you better go check the horses. I can carry the rest of the food in."

With a quick glance around, he could see things were getting busy. "I'm fine. Bud is handling the stock, but I'll need to get over to the pens and help soon. I wanted to talk with you first." He took Maura by the arm and pulled her toward the large oak tree next to where his truck was parked. It was the best he could do for privacy. He looked at her and suddenly his mouth went dry. She was so pretty, dressed in her Wrangler jeans and bright pink Western blouse. She even had on boots.

"You make a mighty pretty cowgirl," he said.

"Thank you. Most of these things are Abby's. The boots." She patted her black Stetson. "And hat."

"They look good on you."

Her smile brightened. "Thank you. I admit, I'm excited about today. I've never been to a rodeo." Her big dark eyes raised to his. "I can't wait to see you ride."

He shook his head. "I hope you're not disappointed. It's been a while since I've ridden in a rodeo. Dylan's the true star in the family."

"I bet you're good, too, and I'll be rooting for you."

His chest suddenly swelled. "Every cowboy wants a girl to cheer him on. Will you be my girl…for today?"

She blinked. "Look, Wyatt, I know you brought me today, but there are so many people—women…beautiful women here. If you happen to see someone that you want to spend time with…"

"I don't care about other woman, Maura, I care about you."

Maura's eyes widened and he kissed the end of her nose.

"Besides, with all the guys around," he said, "I don't want any of them coming on to you. I don't want you dancing with anyone else, or…kissing anyone else." He reached for her, pulled her against him just before his mouth captured hers. She whimpered, but not in protest, and raised her hands to his shoulders and parted her lips, allowing him to deepen the kiss. By the time he broke away, he had trouble drawing air into his lungs.

"That's so you'll only be thinking about me today."

Wyatt marched off, hoping that the kiss had dazed her as much as it had him. Because he didn't know how else to get through to her that he cared about her…a lot.

Two hours later, Maura was sitting in the bleachers next to Abby, Jeff and Kelly, waiting for the festivities to start.

"So what's it like living with Wyatt?" Abby whispered.

Maura tensed, wondering if anyone else heard her friend's question. "I'm not living *with* him, just in the same house."

Abby smiled. "It's kind of nice, isn't it?"

Maura wanted to deny it, wanted to say she hated having a man in the house, but she couldn't. In the beginning the last thing she'd wanted was a man in her life. Now, she looked forward to seeing Wyatt every morning, and every evening, when she returned from work. In fact, she'd been getting up earlier in hopes of running into him before he went out to feed the stock.

Maura glanced at her kids who were busy watching the rodeo clowns. "I thought you were worried about me trusting him too easily."

"That was before I got to know him," Abby admitted. "Besides, Chance, Cade and Travis like him. They're great judges of character. And I see how he treats you, the way he looks at you. The man is smitten.''

Maura smiled to herself. ''To answer your question, yes, it is nice,'' she said. ''And Wyatt is nothing like Darren. He's good to me and to the kids. Is that what you want to hear?''

''So are things getting serious between you two?'' Abby asked.

Maura refused to think about the future. She wasn't going to get her hopes up. How could she expect Wyatt to take on her problems?

''No, nothing is getting serious. I'm just living in his house and when the cottage is repaired, he's renting it to me.''

Abby folded her arms over her chest. ''Well, then, I guess I was mistaken when I saw Wyatt kissing you under the tree earlier.''

Maura felt heat flame her face. ''Okay, we kissed. But it's not going any further.''

''Why not? I mean, if you have feelings for the guy, who's to say you couldn't make a life with him? You *are* divorced.''

''You know it's not that simple, Abby. Darren swore he'd find me.''

''Then tell Wyatt about the threats.'' She lowered her voice. ''If he cares about you as much as I think he does, he won't let anything happen to you and the kids.''

Maura wanted to trust in the future, but would Wyatt hang around if things got too complicated?

Crazy.

That was the only word Wyatt could think of as he climbed the outside railing of the chute where a snorting and kicking Rock-a-Billy was penned. The animal was not happy. Wyatt's old injuries began to ache. He'd never forgotten what a bucking horse could do to a body.

Too late now.

Hearing his name being announced as the next rider, Wyatt got into position. With his legs braced on either side of the railing, he hovered over the animal and slid his rosin-covered glove under the rigging. He shoved his black cowboy hat farther down on his head, then lowered his body onto the bronc. With his nod the gate swung open, causing the crowd to cheer as the horse charged out into the arena.

Billy lowered his head and immediately went into a fast spin, but Wyatt had expected it. When the bronc reared up in a high kick, he felt his entire body jar painfully. Spin and kick. When Billy bucked the second time Wyatt managed to stay on. By the third time, he wasn't so lucky and he landed at an odd angle and was unable to regain his balance. The next buck pitched him high in the air and this time he hit the hard ground.

The buzzer sounded.

Wyatt's survival skills took over. He scrambled to his feet and hurried out of the way of the wayward horse. Out of breath, he made it through the gate and confronted a grinning Chance.

"Hey, that was a damn good ride," Chance said. "And that's one helluva bucking horse you got there."

Wyatt tried to hide the pain in his body and smile. "You think so?" He brushed the dirt from his pants and chaps.

"Man, I don't know anyone who could stay on that animal. But we'll know for sure later on."

Wyatt glanced up in the stands to see Maura coming down the steps toward him.

"Wyatt, are you hurt?"

Not wanting to be in the crowded area, he took her hand and pulled her away from the stands. "No, I'm fine," he said, pleased about her concern.

"Maybe you shouldn't have ridden so soon after your accident."

"The doctor said it was okay," he assured her.

"You're not going to ride again, are you?"

"I doubt it. I didn't last out the eight seconds."

Her gaze moved over him again. "Are you sure that you didn't get hurt?"

"I'll feel a lot better if you'd give me a kiss." He cupped her face between his hands. "It'll help me forget about the pain." Then he lowered his head and touched his mouth to hers, gently, sweetly. He pulled away and smiled. "Oh, darlin', I'm feeling better already."

Maura was feeling pretty good, too. Too good to think about what people would think. Too good to worry about any problems that would stop them from being together. She wanted to be with Wyatt, wanted to feel free to get to know him…to see where it would lead.

"Wyatt, you were great," Jeff said as he ran up to him.

He stepped back from Maura. "Thanks, Jeff, but I'm afraid I'm a little out of practice."

Jeff looked toward the ground. "I wish I could do that," he mumbled.

Wyatt glanced at Maura, then back to the boy. "Well, why don't we sign you up for the kids rodeo?"

Maura felt panic. "Oh, no. Jeff's too young to be on a horse."

"Maura, the kids ride sheep and they wear helmets for protection. I'll be right there with Jeff." His gaze connected with hers. "I won't let anything happen to him."

After having seen this man with her children, Maura knew he spoke the truth. "And I trust you," she said, then turned to her son. "Jeff, listen to Wyatt and do exactly what he tells you."

"I will, Mom," he promised, then hugged her. "I'm gonna win, because Wyatt will teach me." He took Wyatt's hand. "C'mon, we got to go so I can practice."

With a big grin, Wyatt winked at Maura. "I guess I'll catch up with you later. Save a spot for me at the barbecue."

"I will." Maura wanted to go with them, but she'd promised to help with the food. She glanced at her watch just as Abby was coming down the bleachers with her two-year-old son, James, and Kelly.

"One kiss, I'll believe you're just friends. A second kiss, there's no way. The man is crazy for you. And I think you're crazy for him, too."

"I'm still not jumping into anything," Maura swore, but that didn't mean she could stop her growing feelings for Wyatt.

She doubted anything would stop that.

The afternoon had turned out to be so much fun. When Ella had found out that Jeff was riding in the children's rodeo, she sent Maura on her way. She arrived just in time to catch her son's attempt at bareback riding. He lasted a few seconds on the animal before he fell off. Seeing her son lying facedown in the dirt, she wanted to go to him, but Wyatt beat her there. He helped Jeff up and brushed him off as the crowd cheered. For his efforts he won a ribbon and a straw cowboy hat with the Circle B Rodeo band.

Maura had seen so many changes in her children in the past few months, especially in Jeff. He no longer had a bad attitude and wasn't causing problems at school anymore. Most importantly, he no longer asked about going back to Dallas and his father.

Now Maura had another problem. Everything out of her son's mouth was Wyatt this, or Wyatt that. She couldn't help being concerned, but she was selfish enough not to want to give up this time she and the kids had with Wyatt, either. It could all end, though. Darren would never allow her to be with anyone else.

But Darren wasn't going to spoil their good time. Not today. At the picnic area, she and Kelly found a table under a shade tree, making sure there was plenty of room for everyone, including Abby, Cade and their children.

Maura was standing in the food line when Wyatt came up behind her and whispered, "Hey there, beautiful. You want to share a picnic with me?"

She glanced over her shoulder at him. To say he was good-looking didn't begin to cover it. He was a rodeo cowboy and fit right into today's events. He was self-assured and had an easy smile. He shouldn't have worried about people accepting him. He attracted everyone's attention, especially the women.

Females of every age were nearly drooling over him, dressed in his fitted Wrangler jeans stacked over his fancy tooled boots and a starched, royal-blue Western shirt. Including herself.

"Oh, but I promised to eat with the cowboy who brought me." She looked around, enjoying their playful game. "Maybe you've seen him. He's tall and skinny, a little bowlegged." She began to laugh when he poked her ribs.

"I'm not bowlegged."

"And you're not skinny, either." A warm blush flooded her cheeks.

He leaned closer. "So you've been giving me the once-over, huh?"

Heat surged through her and she tried to pull away from his intoxicating scent. She was acting like a teenager. "Not that you haven't noticed that every other woman has, too."

Wyatt refused to let her sidestep his question. "But all I care about is you." He grew serious and whispered, "I can't wait until the dancing starts and I can hold you in my arms."

Maura's pulse raced, so did her uneasiness. "I don't know if we should stay that late. I mean, the kids will be pretty tired by then."

"We'll see," he said. "We'll see."

They continued through the line and piled their plates with as much food as they could handle. Back at the table, Maura assisted Kelly and Wyatt brought Jeff a plate. She'd never before realized how much Wyatt had helped her and the easiness they shared together. Maura didn't miss Abby's eagle eye watching from the end of the table.

Kelly took a bite of her hot dog. "Wyatt, I told Katie Rose that Rock-a-Billy is the prettiest horse at the rodeo. She said that her daddy's horse is the prettiest." She gave him a pouty look.

"Katie's daddy raises horses for show," Wyatt said. "My horses are for the rodeo." He smiled at her. "I'm glad you think Billy is pretty, but he's not a riding horse. He's trained to buck and kick, so you have to promise me that you won't try to ever get close to him."

"I promise," she said. "But I think Raven is a nice horsey."

"But still too big for you," Maura said. "Stick with Sandy."

Cade sat down next to his wife. "You know, Wyatt, Jared and Dana have some good saddle horses, if you're interested in more riding stock. He gives family discounts."

"Maybe I'll look into it."

"And for your information, you can get from the Rocking R to Mustang Valley by horseback. That is, if you want to ride that far." Cade smiled. "Of course, it's well worth it when you get there. Abby and I ride there all the time." He winked at his wife. "It's nice to get away by ourselves, isn't it, honey?"

Kelly refused to be denied attention. "I can ride a pony. Wyatt teached me."

Abby spoke up from the end of the table. "You know, Kelly, we have a pony at our ranch." The woman's green eyes lit up. "Oh, I have an idea, Maura, why don't you let Kelly and Jeff come spend the night so all the kids can go riding in the morning?" She was obviously delighted at her great idea.

"Oh, Mommy, can we go?" Kelly begged.

Her son joined in. "Yeah, Mom, please, I want to go, too."

"Abby, I can't ask you to take on all these kids tonight. You have to be exhausted after today."

"No, really. It's fine." Abby nudged her husband as he ate. "Isn't it fine with us, Cade?"

"Huh? Oh, sure. The more the merrier."

She smiled. "See, now you two can have a free night, even stay late at the dance, or…go home."

Maura was too embarrassed to look at Wyatt, but she admitted to herself it sounded like a wonderful idea.

Wyatt stood on the side of the patio as the band began to play their first song. Maura still hadn't shown up. He was beginning to think that she was hiding from him. Had he come on too strong and scared her off?

Chance came up to him and handed him a beer. "So, how are you liking the festivities so far?"

"It's great. Hank puts on a great rodeo." Wyatt had been surprised at how well organized and professional it was.

Chance took a long pull from his bottle. "Your horses were a great addition to the competition today. Usually we don't have such high caliber stock for our amateur riders. As you could see, not many of us could stay on long."

"I didn't do much better."

"Yeah, but I bet Dylan 'the Devil' Gentry could. What do you think the chances are that he might stop by next year?"

Wyatt hated to disillusion the Randells about Dylan. "I'd like that, too, but it's going to take a lot to convince my brother. He's still upset about me buying the Randell ranch." Wyatt left out the fact that Dylan hadn't returned his calls.

"He'll get over it."

"Maybe. But it didn't sit well with your family at first that I bought the Rocking R."

Chance smiled. "We're over it. My brothers and I didn't want any part of the ranch, so it seems fitting now that you have it, especially since you're bringing the place back to how it used to be. Which leads me into another proposition. How do you feel about helping out with the Mustang Valley Guest Ranch?"

Wyatt jerked his head to Chance. "Help out how?"

Chance shrugged. "We're not sure exactly. You have some prim grazing land on the Rocking R. And at the guest ranch we get a lot of requests for cattle drives.

Why not run a small yearling herd and have people pay you to round them up?''

Wyatt was caught off guard by the offer.

''Maybe you could stop by for a family meeting and work out some of the details. If you're interested…''

Before Wyatt had a chance to speak, they both looked up at Maura, who was coming across the patio. She had changed her clothes. Now, she was wearing a denim skirt and white top covered by a suede vest. Her hair was pulled on top of her head with stands of curls dancing around her face.

''Whoa, Maura sure looks pretty,'' Chance said. ''I guess we'll be continuing this conversation later.'' With that he walked off.

Wyatt barely noticed Chance's departure. His gaze was on Maura as she walked to him.

''Hi,'' she said nervously.

''Hi, yourself, beautiful,'' he said and reached for her hand and led her to the dance floor. He took her in his arms and began the two-step. She stumbled, then with his encouragement, she caught on to the rhythm.

''You're a good dancer,'' he said, wanting to pull her closer.

''I should be, since my mother had me taking lessons since I was three years old. It never made me the prima ballerina that she'd hope for. I never seemed to fulfill any of Mother's expectations.''

Wyatt didn't miss the sadness in her voice. The music ended and a slow song began. He drew Maura close and inhaled her sweetness along with the wonderful feeling of her soft curves against him. Heaven.

''Where do your parents live?''

''The east. New York state.''

''Why didn't you go back there after your divorce?''

She raised her head from his shoulder. The pain reflected in her eyes told him more than her words. "They didn't want me...or the children cluttering up their lives." Her voice softened. "They haven't had anything to do with me since I married Darren."

"Maura, I'm sorry." Wyatt tightened his hold as they moved to the Garth Brooks song, "To Make You Feel My Love."

"I guess we can't choose our families," he said, feeling the softness of her breasts brush against his chest as they moved to the sultry ballad. "But you have the Randells...and me."

She lifted her head again. "Wyatt, I don't want you to feel that you're responsible—"

He placed a finger against her lips. "Don't tell me how to feel, Maura. I know you don't trust men easily and...if I'm coming on too strong, or if I'm speaking out of turn, I'll back away. The last thing I want to do is hurt you, I swear."

She swallowed. "I believe you. It's just there is so much you don't know about my situation."

He danced her toward the corner of the patio, then took her hand and walked to a dark, secluded part of the yard. "Do you trust me, Maura?"

She nodded slowly.

"Do you believe that I care about you and the kids?"

She nodded again and he released a long breath. "Good."

He pulled her into his arms and kissed her. He groaned when she gripped the front of his shirt and held on as she returned his passion. When Wyatt heard people's voice and laughter, he broke off the kiss and pressed his forehead against her. "I think this place is getting too crowded. I want to be alone with you in the worst way.''

He felt her trembling in his arms. "I want that, too." she admitted. Wyatt took her hand and they headed across the patio. Maura didn't have to worry about the children because Abby and Cade had already headed home for the kids' sleepover.

Hours earlier, Bud had loaded the horses into the trailer and taken them back to the Rocking R. All that was left was saying good-night to Hank. They caught up with him along with Chance and Travis and talked a few minutes, then excused themselves and said they'd be leaving.

Silently they walked to the truck. They reached the cab driver's side door and Wyatt lifted Maura in his arms and placed her inside, then slid in next to her.

"Don't move, I don't want you too far away. In fact, I plan to keep you close to me all night."

His gaze met hers in the dark truck, only the moonlight outlined her silhouette. He could feel her tremble. Was she still afraid of him?

"Maura, I want you to know how much I want you. But I'd never force you into anything." He started to move away.

"No, Wyatt, don't leave me." She took hold of his shirt to stop him. "I want to be with you tonight, too."

Chapter Ten

The twenty minute ride to the Rocking R Ranch seemed to take forever. All the while Wyatt kept his hand locked with Maura's until he pulled the truck up next to the back door. Without a word, he unbuckled her safety belt, took her in his arms and kissed her deeply. When he finally tore his mouth away, he drew in needed air. Never in his life had he wanted anyone as much as he wanted Maura.

"Let's go inside," he said, then opened the door and climbed down from the cab. He helped her out and kept her close to his side as they made their way up the porch steps and into the dark kitchen. A tiny light was on over the stove, throwing the room in shadows, but it was enough so he could see her, see the longing in her eyes.

"I had a good time today," he said, suddenly feeling as nervous as an adolescent boy. He released another breath and drew her against him. "God, Maura, I don't want to leave you. Just tell me you feel the same."

"I don't want this night to end, either," she admitted

as she rested her head against his chest. The feel of her soft curves awakened every nerve ending in his body.

Go slow, he warned himself.

But his pulse sped up. When he murmured her name into her hair as he stroked his hand down her back, Maura moved against him restlessly. Her fingers knotted in his shirt front and she turned her face up to his. He felt her breath feather across his cheek, adding fuel to his desire. She raised up on her toes and her lips brushed his. When she pressed her mouth to his, Wyatt forgot his resolve and kissed her.

She whimpered, straining closer to him as he deepened the kiss. Her lips yielded to him. Parted. He dipped his tongue inside, teasing hers into an erotic dance. Suddenly his mind forgot all reason as his body grew warm with need.

His hands roamed over her soft body, bringing her so close she couldn't help but feel his desire. He couldn't get enough of her. He cupped her breasts through her T-shirt, gently squeezing the luscious weight in his hands.

"Oh, Wyatt," she breathed as her hands went to the snaps on his shirt. Once they were opened, she reached inside and caressed his chest. Her touch nearly drove him crazy.

His breathing was ragged. "I want you, Maura, so much."

"I want you, too."

That was all he needed to hear. He swung her up into his arms and carried her to his bedroom off the kitchen. There, he set her down next to the large bed, sliding her along his front, then taking her mouth in another hungry kiss. He moved away and flicked on the small light next to the bed in the sparsely furnished room.

She looked so fragile and shy. "Oh, Maura, if you're not ready... I'll understand."

"No, I want you Wyatt...so much. It's just... I haven't been with anyone else..."

Wyatt cupped her face between his hands, feeling her tremble.

"Not to worry, darlin'. You give me pleasure just looking at you." He touched her hair. "Tonight, I want to fulfill your desires."

Wyatt's promise stole Maura's breath away. And the last thing she wanted to do was pass out before she experienced loving this man. Even if they could never have a future together, she wanted to pretend, just for a while, that it was possible.

"Make love to me, Wyatt," she murmured.

Wyatt stood back, striped off his shirt, then removed his boots and belt. He left on his jeans and returned to her.

He reached out. "May I," he said in a husky voice, "do the honors?"

Unable to find her voice, Maura nodded and he slipped off her vest, then sat her down on the bed and removed her boots. Next came her skirt and top, leaving her in only a bra and panties. She fought not to cover herself, not to let years of abusive conditioning make her feel unattractive. But not tonight. All she had to do was look into Wyatt's eyes, and he told her without words how much he desired her.

"So beautiful." He kissed her and pressed her backward until she rested on the mattress. His mouth left hers and rained kisses along her neck to her chest. He unfastened her bra, baring her breasts to his gaze, but then paused, as if waiting for her to make the next move. For the first time in a long time. Maura wanted a man's hands on her, wanted him to make her feel like a woman.

"Wyatt…touch me," she pleaded.

Wyatt savored Maura's gasp when he cupped her full breast in his hand then he lowered his head and took her nipple into his mouth. She cried out, sinking her fingers into his scalp. He grew more aroused knowing what he was doing to her.

He looked in her eyes as his hand moved over her stomach to the rim of her panties. "Maura, I'm going to stroke and kiss every inch of you…"

She reached up and placed a kiss on his lips, then began to move down to his chest, using her mouth to drive him closer to the edge. "Make love to me."

"Hold that thought." Wyatt groaned, and moved off the bed. He began stripping off his jeans, only thinking about loving Maura. Then suddenly he heard a loud pounding on the back door, then Bud calling his name.

"What the hell? I'll be right back." He walked out, closing the door behind him.

Maura sat up and hugged the sheet against her body on hearing the muffled voices.

Within seconds, Wyatt came back. "Somehow Billy and Stormy got loose and Bud and I have to go after them." He sat in the chair and began pulling on his boots.

She tried to mask her disappointment. "Oh, Wyatt. How did it happen?"

Grabbing his shirt off the floor, he put it on as he walked to the bed. "Bud's not sure, but if we don't chase them down…"

"Of course."

He leaned down and kissed her. "We're not finished here," he whispered. "So don't you go changing your mind, darlin', 'cause I'm going to love you like you've never been loved before. I want you waiting right here—in this bed.''

She could only nod. He kissed her again, sending more warm shivers through her. Then he left.

Maura collapsed back on the pillow with a smile. "I'll be here, Wyatt. I love you…'' she whispered in the empty room as she snuggled into the soft mattress. She closed her eyes a moment, maybe even dosed off when she heard a noise. Maybe he'd forgotten something.

"Wyatt…'' she called.

No answer. She sat up in bed as a strange feeling came over her. Something was wrong. She got up and grabbed one of Wyatt's shirts from the top of the dresser and slipped it on. She'd no sooner finished with the buttons when the door swung open and a figure appeared in the doorway. Panic filled her.

She gasped. "Wyatt…''

"Sorry, bitch, but your lover is long gone.''

Maura's lungs refused to work as she watched Darren Wells stroll into the bedroom. At five foot eight and with his stocky build, he outweighed her by a good fifty pounds. He had dirty blond hair that was too long, and his body odor nearly gagged her.

From years of conditioning and knowing his brutality, she automatically backed away. "What are you doing here?'' Her heart hammered against her ribs as she gripped the edge of the dresser.

"Ah, Maura, is that any way to greet your husband?''

"You aren't my husband,'' she said, trying to sound in control. She prayed Wyatt would appear any second, but now knew that probably wouldn't happen.

He grinned at her, making her stomach clench. "You thought you were rid of me, huh?''

"How did you get...out of jail?"

"Got myself a hotshot lawyer who found a loophole. Seems that the Dallas police didn't follow procedure when they arrested me." His voice turned angry. "And you didn't waste any time finding yourself a lover, did you?"

"What did you do to Wyatt?" Maura demanded. Why hadn't the D.A. called her? she wondered wildly, looking around for a way to escape.

"Let's just say he'll be chasing horses for a long time." He looked around the room. "You have a nice setup here. Too bad you aren't going to be able to stay and enjoy it. Get dressed, bitch. We're going to get the brats and get the hell out of here."

"No, leave the children out of this."

"Can't do that," he told her. "It's the only way I'll keep you in line."

She couldn't go through this again. "I'm not going with you."

He walked toward her, then pulled a gun from the belt of his trousers. "You are, unless you don't want your lover to live."

Maura gasped, then caught her skirt as Darren threw it at her. She dressed as fast as her trembling hands would allow, all the time trying to come up with a plan to get away—and keep Wyatt safe.

"C'mon, quit stalling." Darren grabbed her by her arm and pain shot through her.

Memories of her old life flooded back, but she couldn't let him get control again. She also knew that her ex-husband was going to make her pay for her betrayal, for calling the police on him. She had no doubt that he would hurt her, maybe even kill her. Thank God that Jeff and Kelly were safe with Abby and Cade. She would make sure they stayed that way.

Darren hauled her through the dark house and out the front door. She didn't see a vehicle, but realized that he wouldn't be so stupid as to drive up to the door.

"How did you find out where I was?"

He jerked her along beside him toward the road to the highway. "Simple. Remember that nosy old biddy who lived downstairs, the one who was always calling the police on me? Well, I phoned her and said I was from the D.A.'s office and needed your new address for the file."

He stopped abruptly and she ran into his sweaty body, his sour beer breath nearly made her gag. "Don't you know that you can never get away from me?" His mouth crushed against hers. As never before, she found the strength to fight him. She pummelled her fists into his chest until she broke free. She began to run, praying she could hide in the dark.

She didn't get to the high bushes before he tackled her to the ground, driving the air from her lungs. He pinned her as he smacked her face. She hit him back, scratching and clawing at him. She didn't know how long they struggled before she felt his weight being lifted off of her.

Wyatt! She watched as the two men fought, then Darren rolled away and pulled out his gun. She heard the sound of the hammer being cocked.

"No, Darren, don't!" Maura cried as he aimed the weapon at Wyatt. "I'll go with you, just don't hurt him!"

"Maura, no," Wyatt growled.

Before anything happened, the shrill sound of the sheriff's siren filled the silence. Wyatt caught Darren off guard and lunged at him. The gun went flying. Then Wyatt rammed his fist into Darren's jaw and he dropped to the ground, unconscious.

Wyatt hurried to Maura's side and wrapped his arms around her as the patrol car skidded to a stop, flooding the area with its headlights. The lean built sheriff and a young looking deputy sprang out of the doors with their guns drawn.

"Raise your hands," he demanded.

Wyatt did as he was told. "Sheriff, I'm Wyatt Gentry. I made the 911 call," he said and nodded to the ground. "This is Darren Wells, he tried to kidnap Maura…and held a gun on us both."

The deputy held Darren down and handcuffed him as the sheriff retrieved the gun, then returned to them. "Are you okay?" he asked Maura. "Do you need to go to the hospital?"

"No, I'm fine," she said. "He didn't hurt me."

Wyatt knew she was lying. Her face showed the end result of Darren's fist. "You sure you don't want a doctor to check you out?"

She shook her head. "What about you?"

"I'm fine," he said. "I'm just glad I got here in time."

"It was Darren who let the horses out," she told him.

"I figured something was wrong when I found that the fence had been cut. I called the sheriff thinking someone was stealing the horses. I didn't know Darren was behind it until I came to see if you were safe."

"What about Stormy and Billy?"

"I sent Bud to retrieve them and I came back to make sure you were okay."

"Now that the police are here, maybe you should go and help him."

He shook his head. "I'm not leaving you, Maura." He slipped his arm around her, but she pulled back.

"I'm fine, Wyatt. I just want to see my children." Tears flooded her eyes. "I need to know that they're safe."

Wyatt pulled the cell phone from his pocket. "Here, call Abby and make sure."

Maura took the phone and walked a few feet away to make the call. Wyatt wanted to stay with her, but she seemed to want to be alone so he took the opportunity to talk to the sheriff. "You have to keep Wells locked up. Look what he did to her face."

"I don't see it as a problem. We ran a check on Wells as we drove out here. Seems he's been ID'd for an armed robbery in Dallas. If we're lucky that will be enough to put him away for a long time. But I'm gonna need a statement from Mrs. Wells on the assault, which will add to the charges."

"They're no longer married," he snapped, then realizing how possessive he'd become of Maura. "Sorry, it's been a rough night. Could she come in tomorrow morning?"

"No problem. We have plenty to hold him." The sheriff went back to the car and drove off.

Maura returned to Wyatt and handed him the phone. "Jeff and Kelly are asleep, but I need to see them. Please, can you take me there?"

"Sure. I can run you by for a while."

"No, Wyatt, I'm not coming back here. I'll be staying with Abby and Cade." She couldn't meet his eyes. "I'm not sure what's going to happen after that."

Wyatt's gut tightened. "Maura... I care about you. I thought that you and I have something between us."

She looked at him. "Right now I have to concern

myself with my children and surviving. I can't drag you into my mess of a life.''

He stepped closer. ''What if I want to be there, to help you?''

She shook her head. ''I have to help myself.'' This time she met his gaze. ''Please, Wyatt, try to understand. I have nothing to give you.'' She swung around and hurried off toward the house.

Wyatt just stood there, feeling as if his heart had been ripped from his chest. She was wrong. Maura had everything to give him, everything that mattered to him.

It had been one week since Darren Wells had shown up at the Rocking R Ranch. One week since Maura had moved out, since he had last seen Jeff and Kelly. And he missed them like hell.

He should be spending his time on the business. Bud was at a rodeo in New Mexico. Wyatt had no desire to go along, even though he was going stir crazy. He saddled Raven and headed out, following the directions Cade had given him, he rode off. The stallion pranced, eager to run. Wyatt finally let him loose and they took off across the open pasture.

Twenty minutes later Wyatt slowed Raven when they reached the group of trees at the edge of Mustang Valley. He'd been here once before and remembered the place's peacefulness and beauty. At the crest of the rise, he looked down at the trees lining the creek. Off in the distance he could see the shadows of the cabins partially hidden in the shrubs. On the other side, in the hills, he spotted a large structure. The two-story home was all natural-stained wood and the back side was nearly all glass. Travis and Josie's home. He turned his attention back to the pasture and he found the herd of mustangs in the high grass.

Silently, he climbed off Raven and led the horse to the water's edge. They both took a drink, careful not to disturb the serene atmosphere. He watched in fascination as two mustang studs began to whinny and nip at each other. Before long, the two were all out fighting over the buckskin mare. Finally the dominate male ran the younger one off. So engrossed in the action, Wyatt didn't hear Hank come up behind him.

"It's still survival of the fittest," the rancher said. "And it's as old as time, males fighting over a female." He studied Wyatt. "I thought maybe you'd be doing the same."

Wyatt frowned. "She won't see me."

"Maura thinks she's doing the noble thing, saving you from all the trouble in her life. Plus, she's just plain scared."

Wyatt clenched his fists. "She didn't make the mess to begin with. That bastard of an ex-husband did that all on his own."

"Maybe you need to convince her of that."

He wished he had the chance. "How can I when she doesn't want to see me?"

Hank cocked an eyebrow. "Well, she may have said that, but I know for a fact she isn't happy these days. The kids aren't in much better shape." He pushed his hat back. "But, son, in good conscience I can't allow you to go over there if your intentions aren't honorable."

Marriage. It had been all he'd thought about since Maura left him. Being alone these past days he realized the home he'd always wanted meant nothing if he couldn't share it with Maura. "I want to give her every-

hing she's never had, a home for her and Jeff and Kelly.
Yes, I love her.''

The older rancher gave him a sly smile. "Now those
hree words may just change her mind, if she knows that
you want it to be permanent between you. That is what
you're talkin' about, isn't it?''

Wyatt nodded. "Yeah, I guess it is.''

Hank nodded in approval. "Then she better be the one
you're tellin'. Women need to hear it all spelled out.
You know, with pretty flowers and all the fancy words.''

Wyatt wasn't good with words, but he refused to let
Maura walk out of his life, not without a fight. "Do you
happen to know where Maura might be today?''

"Sure do. When I left Cade and Abby's place just a
while ago, she was sittin' on the porch looking pretty,
and mighty lonely.'' Hank pointed toward the west. "If
you head up the rise, you'll have no trouble finding the
way. The trail will take you right there.''

"Thanks.'' Wyatt swung up onto Raven's back,
tugged on the reins and shot off in the direction of the
Rocking R. This was the first time in a week he felt a
glimmer of hope.

Chapter Eleven

Maura sat on the porch and watched Kelly and Katie Rose play with their dolls off in a corner. It was a cool autumn day and Maura had the day off from the Yellow Rose. In a way she wished she could work. At least it kept her busy so she wouldn't have so much time to think about how much she missed Wyatt...and remember. Remember how it felt to have him hold her, to kiss her. She closed her eyes recalling the night they'd nearly made love.

"Thinking about a certain sexy cowboy who lives up the road?"

Maura's eyes shot open to find Abby sitting in the chair next to hers.

"No," she lied. "I have too many other things on my mind, like my future and finding a place to live. We've imposed on you enough."

"Our house has plenty of room," Abby insisted. "Besides, Cade told you that you can move into the foreman's house." She took Maura's hand. "You don't have to run anymore, Maura. Darren is going to prison, and with the armed robbery charge, he's not getting out for a long time. Texas has tough laws. So you and the kids can have a life, a good life. Don't waste any more time on your ex.''

"It's thanks to you, Abby. You and your family took us in when I had nowhere else to go.''

She smiled. "Everyone needs help now and then. You've paid me back many times. You've made the Yellow Rose prosper with your creative designs. But you need to think about yourself, think about the man you love.''

Maura wished she could give into her feelings. "Who says I love him?''

Her friend raised an eyebrow. "You're denying it?''

Maura knew it was useless. "Sometimes love isn't enough. How can I ask another man to take on a family, plus all my baggage? Jeff or Kelly might have problems because of their father's abuse. I'm still in counseling.''

"So am I. And because sometimes love is the only thing that gets you through. Besides, life has no guarantees,'' Abby stressed. "If I hadn't taken a chance and let Cade back into my life, I wouldn't be with the man I love. And Brandon wouldn't have his daddy. I definitely wouldn't have Jamie.''

Maura wanted so badly to believe Abby, but the fear was still with her. Besides, Wyatt hadn't made any indication that he wanted her...forever. "If he wants me, why hasn't he come?''

"As I recall, you asked him for some time.''

Maura started to speak when she spotted a horse and rider coming through the pasture toward the house. She immediately recognized the large black stallion and the man. Her heart raced. It was Wyatt.

Wyatt slowed Raven as he approached the large ranch house. Nerves had his pulse pounding in his ears. He touched the brim of his hat at the two women seated on the porch, but before he could get any closer, little Kelly came running down the steps to greet him. He climbed off his horse and swung the child up in his arms.

"Wyatt! Wyatt! You came!"

"Yes, I did.

She pouted. "I missed you." Then her voice lowered to a whisper. "Jeff and me want to live at your house, but Mama says we can't." Her eyes teared up. "Can you tell her it's okay?"

Wyatt glanced toward the porch to see that Cade had joined the ladies on the porch. He hadn't planned on a crowd. "I'll do my best."

Suddenly Jeff came tearing out of the barn. "Wyatt, you're here!" the boy cried.

"How you been doin', partner? You being good for your mother?"

Jeff nodded. "I got an A on my printing, too."

Kelly wasn't going to be left out. "I've been good, too. And I drawed you lots of pictures."

"Why didn't you come for us?" Jeff asked. "Don't you care about us?"

"I care a lot about you and your sister," Wyatt tried to assure them. He tugged on Kelly's blond ponytail, then looked over his shoulder to see Maura watching them.

"Do you love us?" Kelly asked. "Do you love Mama?"

Wyatt couldn't find his voice and nodded.

"Then marry Mom," Jeff said.

These kids didn't mess around. He decided maybe he

should plead his case to them before he faced Maura. He set Kelly down.

"Come on, you two," he said as he tugged Raven by the reins and all of them walked the short distance to the water trough. As the horse drank Wyatt turned to the children.

"Yes, I want to marry your mother. And I want to be your dad, too." He watched as two pairs of eyes widened.

"Can we live with you forever?" Kelly gasped.

He nodded.

"Oh, boy!" the girl cheered and Wyatt quickly touched his finger to her lips to quiet her. She lowered her voice. "I want you to be my daddy."

"You love us?" Jeff asked.

Wyatt swallowed as placed his hand on Jeff's shoulder. "Yeah, I love you." He saw the child's hesitant look. "Jeff, I can't promise you that I won't get angry with you and your sister, but I'll never raise a hand to either of you." Wyatt thought about his own stepfather's abusive behavior. He'd never treat any child that way.

"I know you won't," Jeff said so confidently. "Will you teach me to play baseball? And can I ride Raven when I'm older?"

Wyatt had trouble speaking. "I'd planned on it."

Kelly spoke up, "And will you read me stories at night?"

"It will be my pleasure, princess. Now, you two need to give me some time with your mother…alone. I'd like to take her back to the ranch so we can talk. So I can tell her how much I care about her. Is that all right?"

They both nodded enthusiastically.

"I can watch Kelly," Jeff offered. "We'll be good for Abby."

"Great, son, because I'm going to need all the help I can get." He patted the boy's shoulder. "Remember, it's a surprise."

Kelly cupped her mouth and whispered, "Give Mommy kisses. She likes kisses." Then she ran off with her brother.

Wyatt smiled. At least he had the kids on his side. "I'll do my best," he promised, recalling the feel of Maura's mouth under his. He sucked in a breath to curb the direction of his thoughts, then led Raven toward the porch.

"Hello, Maura, Abby, Cade. Maura, do you think I can talk with you a minute? Alone."

She hesitated, then came down the steps. He couldn't help but notice the weight she'd lost and the dark circles under her eyes, those big, beautiful eyes. At least there were no remaining traces of bruises.

"How are you doing?"

"I'm fine," she said.

"Good." He felt awkward and glanced off to where the kids were playing on the tire swing that hung on the huge oak.

"Kelly and Jeff seem to be doing well," she said. "I hate to think of what would have happened if they'd been at the house when…"

"But they weren't," Wyatt stressed. "They were safe and they'll be safe from now on."

He took a step closer, aching to touch her, to take her in his arms. To hold her and erase her pain, her fears. Instead, he asked. "When are you and the kids moving back to the house?"

She didn't say anything for several seconds. "I don't think that's such a good idea. I mean, I can't keep imposing on you indefinitely."

"You weren't imposing, Maura, not then and not now," he said. "I want you to come back…to give us a chance."

A hundred times Maura had thought about the night they'd nearly made love. The night Wyatt gave her a glimpse of paradise. She loved this man beyond belief, but…she also needed to learn to rely on herself. No matter how wonderful Wyatt might be, she wasn't ready to trust another man.

"Come back with me to the ranch now. Just to talk," he coaxed.

Looking into those mesmerizing blue eyes of his, Maura felt her resolve slipping. No. She straightened. "I can't now, Wyatt. Maybe after the kids and I get settled."

"When will that be? Never? That's a cop out and you know it. But if you think that's all there is between us, I can't change that."

Maura wasn't frightened of Wyatt's anger, just disappointed when he took hold of the reins and climbed on Raven. He was giving up.

"I can't force you, Maura, but I won't hang around where I'm not wanted, either." The horse shifted sideways. "Just let me know where you want the rest of your things sent." With one last look, he kicked the horse's sides and took off. Maura ached to go after him. She loved him, but knew she couldn't give him what he needed. So all she could do was watch as he rode past the corral and out across the open field.

Suddenly her attention changed when she caught a small figure running after the horse and rider. It was Jeff. Maura watched as the six-year-old yelled and waved frantically to Wyatt. When the rider didn't stop, Jeff changed direction and cut through the fenced pasture.

Maura's heart went to her throat and she started after her son.

Wyatt heard someone calling him and glanced over his shoulder to find Jeff racing through the field waving at him. He slowed his horse, then swung him around to go back to the boy. Suddenly Jeff tripped and fell to the ground, but he didn't get up. Wyatt felt panic and kicked Raven's side and they shot off. The horse jumped the low fence, making his way through the grass to the injured boy. Then Raven whinnied and reared up in distress.

"Whoa, boy." Alerted to danger, Wyatt patted the animal's neck. Jeff was about twenty feet away where he'd fallen and hit a rock. The large rock seemed to be home to a Texas rattler, who now was about five feet from the boy's still body.

Wyatt swallowed back the bile in his throat and slowly climbed off the horse. He could see that the child's head was bleeding, but worse, he was coming to. With Jeff's whimper, the snake sounded his rattle.

"Jeff," Wyatt spoke in a quiet, soothing voice. "Don't move, partner. I know you're hurt, but you have to pretend to be asleep. Trust me, I won't let anything happen to you."

Maura was running as fast as she could to keep up with Cade. When they reached Wyatt, she saw her son lying motionless on the ground.

"Jeff," she cried with what little breath she had left.

Wyatt held up his hand to stop them. Cade grabbed her to keep her from going any closer. A rattling sound alerted Maura to a snake dangerously near Jeff. "Oh, God," she gasped.

Cade held her back. "Maura, let Wyatt handle it."

"Please, Wyatt, help him," she begged, feeling helpless. "Please…"

"I will." Wyatt backed up slowly to Raven, then opened the flap on his saddlebag. He took out a knife and pulled the long blade from its sheath. Maura's heart pounded as she could only watch Wyatt release a breath and take aim. With a skilled flick of the wrist, the blade went sailing through the air and impaled the snake to the earth. Then there was only silence.

No sooner had Cade released her than she took off to her son. Wyatt was already there, checking for injuries. "Hey, partner," he said. "You did good." He ran his hands over Jeff's limbs as Maura knelt beside her son.

"Oh, Jeff," she said, fighting tears. "Are you hurt?"

"My head." He grimaced, then said to her, "Did you see Wyatt, Mom? He killed the snake."

"You did a good job, partner," Wyatt said, as he looked into the boy's eyes, checking the pupils. "You did exactly what I told you and stayed quiet."

"'Cause I knew you'd save me." Jeff tried to sit up. "Can I see the snake?"

Cade got off his cell phone. "I'll save it for later, Jeff. We need to get you checked out." He looked at Wyatt. "Good job with the knife."

Wyatt shrugged. "I've had a little practice."

Just then Cade's ranch foreman, Charlie, drove up in the truck. Wyatt relinquished Raven to Charlie's care, lifted Jeff into the back seat beside Maura, then climbed in the front beside Cade and they all headed to the emergency room.

An hour later, the doctor had examined Jeff and diagnosed with a slight concussion. He'd put a bandage on the cut on his head and told Maura to periodically check his pupils for the next twenty-four hours, then bring him back tomorrow. When she brought Jeff out to the waiting room she found Wyatt still there. Tears welled in her eyes. He hadn't left them.

Wyatt looked down at Jeff. "Looks like the doctor is sending you home."

"Yeah, but I have a concussion. I have to stay awake all night."

Wyatt smiled and Maura realized how hungry she'd been to see it, even if it wasn't directed at her. "Well, maybe you should lay in bed anyway," Wyatt said. "Just to rest."

Jeff nodded then hugged him. "Thanks for saving me, Wyatt."

"Any time, partner," he said putting his arms around Jeff. It dawned on her that she'd never once seen Darren hug his son.

"Well, I've got to get back to the ranch." Wyatt stood and looked at Cade. "Bud's waiting outside for me. Would it be all right to leave Raven at your place until the morning?"

"No problem," Cade said.

Wyatt knelt down in front of Jeff. "You take it easy for the next few days, but that doesn't mean you have to give your mom a bad time."

"I'll be good," he said, then leaned closer to Wyatt. "Are you going to talk to Mom about...you know?"

"I don't think now is the right time," he said.

Jeff looked disappointed. "But you will, right?"

He hugged the boy. "Yeah, I will," he promised.

Wyatt stood and nodded to Maura, then headed for the door. Before exiting, he turned around and their eyes met and she ached to call him back. Then it hit her that he was giving her what she wanted. Wyatt was walking out of her life...forever.

Cade came up to her. "You ready to go?

Afraid to speak, she could only nod.

Cade lifted Jeff in his arms, then placed an arm across her shoulders. They arrived at the car and put the boy in the back. Cade walked her around to the passenger side, but before she got in, she asked, "Am I doing the right thing with Wyatt?"

He pulled off his hat and ran a hand through his hair. "Only you can answer that, Maura" he said. "If you're worried that he'll be like your ex, don't be. We Randells talk big, but we don't have a mean bone in our bodies, unless you mess with our family. Then we'll fight you until our last breath." He glanced at Jeff in the back seat of the truck. "I saw that fierce look in Wyatt's eyes when your boy was lying on the ground. There was no doubt that the man would have gone after that rattler bare handed to protect him. Jeff knew it, too." Cade blinked several times. "Wyatt is definitely a Randell. And I mean that in a good way. My brothers and I are the new generation. We don't walk out on those we love."

Maura smiled despite her pain.

Cade went on to say, "I believe Wyatt came to San Angelo for one reason—to find family. I think he got more than he bargained for. He's crazy about you and your kids."

The back window came down and Jeff leaned out. "Yeah, Mom. Wyatt loves us. He said so."

Maura's chest tightened at her son's words. How she wanted to hear those words from Wyatt. "I'm so confused."

"We're talking about how you feel, Maura," Cade said. "And if you're not ready…" He leaned toward her. "But ask yourself this, why do you so easily trust the man with your child…but not your heart?"

Chapter Twelve

Two days later, Maura sat on the edge of the cold, metal chair inside the jail's visitors' room. Her palms were sweating, her pulse pounding in her ears as she watched the guard escort in Darren Wells. Looking at the heavyset man with greasy blond hair, she couldn't imagine ever loving him. A long time ago she had, before he started abusing her. She shut her eyes to blank out the bad memories, wanting only to remember that he was the father of her children.

One thing was for sure, she wasn't going to allow him to control her life. Not anymore.

"Well, well, if it isn't my loving wife." Darren sat down across from her at the table, only a high Plexiglas partition separating them.

"I'm no longer your wife. Our divorce was final months ago."

"That'll change," he assured her. "I'll be getting out of here."

Maura's breathing stopped, but she tried not to react.

"You're not getting out of here any time soon," she insisted. "I talked to the D.A. about pressing charges of kidnapping and abuse. Between that and the robbery, you'll be in prison for years."

He leaned forward and gave her a threatening look that used to have her trembling. She wasn't trembling now.

"If you know what's good for you, Maura, you better not do that."

She met his gaze defiantly. "No, I should have done it years ago. I should have protected my children from you, protected myself from you. I'm a person, Darren." She sat up straighter, feeling her strength grow. "You had no right to lay a hand on me. I'm here to tell you that you never will again."

"You better watch it, bitch," he growled. "You don't know when I'll come and get you."

She didn't even flinch at his threat, that in itself made her smile. "Well, I'll be waiting. I'm not afraid of you, Darren. You can't hurt me anymore."

He leaned back in his chair. "So you're going to rely on lover boy?"

"No, I'm relying on myself. I'm stronger now. You're never going to control me again." She stood, seeing his surprised expression. "If you have any decency left, you'll do what's right for your children and relinquish your claim to them. Give Jeff and Kelly a chance at a life." She turned and walked out of the room, feeling as if she could breath again.

She was finally free. She could do anything. Have anything. She laughed, then it died away. All she'd ever wanted just might be out of her reach. Or was it? Maybe the man she loved would be willing to give her a second chance.

* * *

Maura pulled her car by the back door at the Rocking R Ranch. When she glanced up at the beautiful white house, her heart ached, remembering when she'd first came here to live. She loved the house back then, she still loved it. But the man who lived inside was who she wanted. She only had to convince him to hear her out.

Before she'd left to come here, Cade had encouraged her to speak her mind, tell Wyatt how she felt. Make him understand how much she cared about him and that she needed him in her life. So did her children. Jeff and Kelly told her not to come back without Wyatt. Maura took a calming breath and picked up the special floral bouquet from the seat and got out of the car.

At the back door, she knocked, but hearing no answer, she stepped into the kitchen and called for Wyatt. There was no reply, just the sound of music. The first thing Maura noticed was the smell of paint, then saw that the walls were a new bright yellow. Not only that, the knotty pine cabinets had been refinished and stained, and white tile had replaced the old battered countertops. She looked down at the floor to see that was also new.

Maura's curiosity took her into the dining room to find it had also been transformed during her two-week absence. The once empty space had been painted the "luscious moss" color she'd chosen and there was a long oak table and six high-back chairs. She ran her fingers along the antique sideboard in awe.

What had Wyatt done?

The music grew louder and Maura followed the voice of Tim McGraw into the living room. She peeked her head around the corner to find Wyatt in the middle of room, busy pushing a roller over the prepped walls. Her gaze moved over his paint-spattered jeans and a once-white T-shirt that hugged his broad shoulders and chest. As if he sensed her presence, he turned and looked at her.

Her breath caught as his gaze moved over her. She tingled from head to toe, praying that he wouldn't reject her. His mouth tugged at a smile which gave her encouragement. "Hello, Wyatt."

"Maura. What are you doing here?"

Wyatt knew immediately he'd said the wrong thing. He set down the roller and wiped off his hands. The last thing he wanted to do was make her feel unwelcome, especially when he'd been praying she'd want to see him. "I mean, I didn't know you were coming by." He gestured around. "As you can see, the place is a mess."

"It looks nice. I hardly recognize the kitchen."

"Yeah, I had someone come in and redo the cabinets and counters. Do you like them?" He was rambling like a teenager.

"Yes, they did a wonderful job."

Wyatt watched her move around the room. She looked good, damn good. She had on a pair of dark pleated slacks showing off her tiny waist. A snowy white blouse made her look businesslike, yet feminine. Her soft blond hair was curled up on the ends and draped behind her small ears. A strand clung to her cheek, and he had to fight to keep from brushing it away. He glanced at the flowers in her hands.

"Who are the flowers for?"

"Oh…ah…they're for you." She held out the bouquet to him. "I wanted to thank you for helping Jeff."

"You don't have to thank me, Maura. I would never let anything happen to him."

"I know." Tears welled in her eyes. "Without you, I don't want to think about what could have happened."

He shook his head. "Then don't. Jeff is fine." He wanted more than her gratitude.

Wyatt took the colorful flowers and walked into the kitchen. She followed him. He opened the cupboard and found a glass vase. At the sink, he added water and set the assortment of flowers inside, then carried it to the table.

"These are really nice. I've never gotten flowers before," he said, seeing that Maura looked as if she were about to bolt out the door. He couldn't let her do that. "Is it true that each flower has some special meaning?"

She shrugged. "I guess."

"Come on, Maura. Surely you know what kind of flowers to suggest…say for someone who wants something for their mother, brother, or sister…or their lover…" He held her gaze, refusing to let her look away. "Did you pick certain flowers because the bouquet was for me?"

She managed a nod. "The daffodils stand for respect," she began, pointing to each flower. "The blue hyacinth, for kindness, and the pussy willows are for friendship."

"What about the roses, Maura?" he asked, hoping she was trying to tell him of her feelings. "What do they stand for?" There were white, pink, yellow, and red roses. Their fragrance made him light-headed, but not as much as Maura's presence.

"The yellow rose stands for friendship." She came to the table and touched each flower, then moved to the next one. "The pink for grace and beauty." Her fingers trembled as she stroked each petal. "The white is for unity, and worthiness."

"You're worthy of anyone, Maura," he said.

Maura looked up at Wyatt and swallowed back the

dryness in her throat. It was now or never. If she wanted this man, she had to be the one to take the chance. His blue eyes locked with hers as her heart pounded in her chest. Then she pulled the red rose and ivy from the bouquet and held it out to Wyatt. "The red is for passion and…love."

"What else does it mean, Maura?"

"Trust. It stands for trust. And I trust you…"

Wyatt took the flower from her and placed it on the table. He lowered his head and touched his lips to hers, then pulled back. "You know what else it means?"

She nodded, but remained silent.

So he spoke, "It means…I love you, Maura. I love you."

"Oh, Wyatt…" Maura's twined her arms around his neck. "I love you, too," she whispered, just before she pulled his mouth down to meet hers in a searing kiss.

Wyatt finally broke off the kiss. "Tell me again." he said.

"I love you." Tears flooded her eyes. "I love you. I'm sorry that I didn't trust you—"

He stopped her words. "No, I didn't give you enough time. Just because I knew immediately how much I wanted you didn't mean you were feeling the same."

She laughed through her tears. "How can you say that when I nearly blurted out the words the night we were together…the night we almost made love? Then Darren showed—"

"No, Maura, you don't need to bring up what happened."

She kissed his fingers and removed them. "It's okay, Wyatt. I don't need you to protect me from Darren. I went to see him, and I told him that he wasn't going to control my life anymore."

He cocked an eyebrow. "You went to the jail?"

"I wanted to come to you with no ghosts from the past. No fears. I didn't want my past stopping us from having a future together." Her eyes met his. "That is, if you still want me."

He pulled her against him. "I haven't stopped wanting you from the first night I saw you waving that rifle at me. When I offered you and the kids the place to live, believe me, it was purely selfish on my part. I wanted you more than any woman I'd ever known. I want to take away all your sadness, Maura. Erase every bad memory in your past, and make it all perfect."

She smiled at him. "That's nice to know."

"Then marry me, Maura Wells. Let me take care of you and the kids."

When she shook her head and he felt his gut knot in agony. "No, Wyatt. If I'm going to be your wife, I want to be an equal partner in our marriage. We'll take care of each other."

He broke out into a grin. "I wouldn't have it any other way. I love you being independent, but not so much that you don't need me."

"Oh, I need you, Wyatt. I just don't want to use you as my crutch. I want to be your wife more than anything, but I'd like to keep working." Her eyes locked with his. "I want to have your child."

He swallowed several times trying to hold his emotions in check over her words. "Oh, Maura. I came here to San Angelo, looking for my father, wondering why he never wanted me. All my life, my stepfather told me that I wasn't good enough to be his son. So I was going to show him. I was sure that all I needed was my own ranch to be happy." He cupped her face in his hands. "Then I found you and Jeff and Kelly. It wasn't until you walked out that I realized this place isn't a home without…love.''

He lowered his head and captured her mouth. He parted her lips, then dipped his tongue inside to taste her, to savor her. He wrapped his arms around her body and pulled her closer, letting her know his desire.

They finally broke apart. ''You want to start working on the baby now?'' He was halfway teasing.

''Don't tempt me,'' Maura said. ''But I think we better go tell Jeff and Kelly the news. You know, it isn't easy being parents.''

''I know, but we can give them the one important thing. We're going to stand together and give them a lot of love.''

She moved closer. ''Maybe you could start with convincing their mother.''

Wyatt lowered his head to hers. ''My pleasure.''

Epilogue

Seated atop Raven, Wyatt led the riders down the steep rise and into the valley below. He looked over his shoulder to see his new wife of three months on her mare, Trudi. Next came Kelly on Sandy, then Jeff followed up the rear on his small mare, Tawny, a present for his seventh birthday and a report card that had straight A's.

"We can have our picnic beside the creek," Wyatt suggested, then climbed off Raven, helping Maura and Kelly. Jeff was already off his mount and smiling. The boy was a natural rider.

"Can we see the ponies?" Kelly begged.

"If they come to the valley," Wyatt said. "Sometimes when people are here they're shy about coming around."

The girl sat down on the blanket Maura had spread on the grass. "I'll be real quiet," she whispered.

"Why don't you two sit here and eat your sandwiches and watch for them," Maura said. "I want to talk to your dad."

Wyatt got a thrill being called by his new title. He still couldn't believe that Darren Wells signed away his rights to the children. So the man had some decency and Wyatt had two wonderful kids.

Maura took hold of her husband's hand and took him off toward a group of trees and away from the ears of the children. It had been wonderful being a family, but they also cherished their time alone. That was mostly late at night after Jeff and Kelly had gone to sleep. Wyatt would take her into the newly decorated bedroom and he'd make love to her, so tenderly that it would bring tears to her eyes. He'd made the bad years disappear, and the loneliness a thing of the past. Every day she counted her blessings that she and the children found him.

Wyatt sat down at the base of the tree and seated Maura between his legs. They faced the valley, appreciating the beautiful scenery. "How much time do you think we have before they interrupt us?" he teased her, then placed a kiss against her temple.

Maura tipped her head back to look at him. "Not much, I suspect. But don't worry, that will change. There will come a day when they'll want to deny knowing us."

Wyatt slapped his chest, looking heartbroken. "Not my Kelly. She'd never deny me. I'm just worried about how to keep the boys away from her. She's going to be just as gorgeous as her mother."

Maura was touched. "You make me feel beautiful," she told him.

"And you make me feel…needy." He nuzzled her neck crossing his arms under her breasts as he whispered in her ear, "You think the kids will fall asleep so I can make love to my wife? Maybe I can convince you it's time to have a baby."

Maura sucked in a breath, feeling a tingle race through her body. They'd talked about waiting, but she wanted Wyatt's child more than her next breath. "You wouldn't have to work too hard talking me into that."

His piercing blue eyes met hers. "Really?"

"Oh, Wyatt. Of course I want *your* child…so much."

She watched the emotions play across his handsome face. "I love you," he whispered then placed a tender kiss on her lips.

Maura reached up and took a teasing nibble from his tempting mouth. "I hope you feel the same when I get out of bed in the middle of the night for my cravings," she said.

"I wouldn't mind at all," he promised her. "I like spoiling my lady. How about I bring you back here later and show you how much?"

With a groan, Maura turned in his arms as his mouth captured hers. This time the kiss was heated by passion and need. No doubt in her mind that making a baby with Wyatt was going to be a most enjoyable experience.

Wyatt couldn't believe how his life had changed since coming to Texas. He thought that buying the ranch would be the home he'd always longed for, thinking that a structure would stop his loneliness. He soon realized that without Maura and kids, his life wasn't complete.

Wyatt also had his extended family, the Randells, and now he was a partner in Mustang Valley Guest Ranch. He had agreed to run a herd of cattle for roundups, something else to offer the ranch guests. Hank Barrett had given him a start with two bulls and a dozen heifers. By next year they would have cattle on the Rocking R just like in the day of their grandfather, John Randell. He finally had roots and a family.

The kids' voices drew his attention and he saw a lone

rider coming down the rise. It was Cade. "Forget about coming back here, this place has too much traffic."

Wyatt stood, taking Maura's hand as they walked back. "Cade. What are you doing here? I thought you were in Dallas."

"Got back this morning," his half brother said. "Wyatt, I just got a call from your mother, Sally. I hate to bring you bad news, but it seems your brother, Dylan, had a bull-riding accident."

Wyatt's heart stopped. "Is he alive?"

"Yes, but I won't lie to you. It's serious."

Maura touched his arm. "You have to go to him, Wyatt. Then when he's well enough, bring him home. We'll help him get through this together."

Wyatt hugged Maura to him. She was his strength… his life. This was what he'd always longed for. Now, if he could only convince Dylan how important family was, too.

* * * * *

Look for Dylan "The Devil" Gentry's story,
DYLAN'S LAST DARE,
coming in March 2004,
only from
Patricia Thayer and Silhouette Romance!

SILHOUETTE *Romance*®

presents

THE SECRET PRINCESS
by Elizabeth Harbison
(Silhouette Romance #1713)

Once small-town bookseller Amy Scott had completed
her transformation from plain Jane to regal princess,
would she still need her handsome royal tutor?

Available March 2004 at your favorite retail outlet.

SILHOUETTE *Romance*®

presents

MAJOR DADDY
by Cara Colter
(Silhouette Romance #1710)

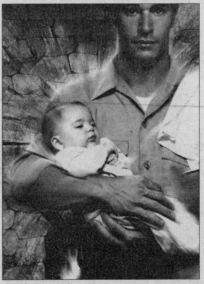

When Major Cole Standen retired, he figured he'd quit
the rescuing business for good. Then five irresistible
tykes—and their sweet and sexy auntie Brooke—
turned up on his doorstep, desperate for his help.
Now, knee-deep in diapers and baby bottles, the
major was suddenly picturing himself with a brood
of his own...and beautiful Brooke as his bride!

Available March 2004 at your favorite retail outlet.

COMING NEXT MONTH

#1710 MAJOR DADDY—Cara Colter
When five adorable, rambunctious children arrived on reclusive
Cole Standen's doorstep, his much needed R and R was thrown
into upheaval. But just when things were back to the way he
liked them (ie. under his control!), Brooke Callan, assistant to the
children's famous mother, arrived. Could Brooke and the brood
of miniature matchmakers rescue this hero's wounded heart?

#1711 DYLAN'S LAST DARE—Patricia Thayer
The Texas Brotherhood
Pregnant physical therapist Brenna Farren was not going to let
her newest patient, handsome injured bull rider Dylan Gentry,
give up on his recovery *or* talk her into entering a marriage of
convenience with him! But soon she found herself in front of a
judge exchanging I dos—and getting a whole different kind of
"physical therapy" from her heartthrob husband!

#1712 AN HEIRESS ON HIS DOORSTEP—
Teresa Southwick
If Wishes Were…
Jordan Bishop fantasized about being a princess and living in
a palace. But when her secret birthday wish was answered
with…*a kidnapping,* she was rescued by the sexiest innocent
bystander she'd ever seen. She found herself in his castle—
and in the middle of a *big* misunderstanding! Could the love-
wary Texas oil baron who saved the day be Jordan's prince?

#1713 THE SECRET PRINCESS—Elizabeth Harbison
The princess was alive! And she was none other than small-
town bookstore owner Amy Scott. Despite her protests, Crown
Prince Wilhelm insisted the skeptical American beauty return
to Lufthania with him. But while Amy was sampling the royal
lifestyle, Wil found himself wanting to sample Amy's sweet kisses.…

SRCNM0204